Kenya Days,
Moonlit Nights

A novel inspired by our times in
Kenya, East Africa

Bhupendra Brahmabhatt

TSL Publications

Published in Great Britain in 2018
By TSL Publications, Rickmansworth

ISBN: 978-1-912416-21-9

Cover: Jem Butcher

Dedication

To my late parents,

Rasiklal Chunilal & Sushilaben Rasiklal
Brahmabhatt,

and to all my fellow East Africans.

FOREWORD

The following pages are a homage to the golden days of the East African Asian and the lifestyle in that part of the world. Thus, although the setting is Kenya, it could as well apply to the other two territories, Uganda or Tanzania, as the lifestyle then was very similar.

It is a novelistic account of young Shekhar Vakil's days in Kenya between the post-war 1940s and the mid-seventies.

I spent nearly two decades of my life in that glorious country, and have drawn on some of my own experiences; however, very few of us, wish as we might, are able to carry out an existence as exciting as that of an Ernest Hemingway or a Jim Corbett, the writer/adventurers. Indeed, some of us have rightly been accused of not even *seeing* enough of those countries whilst we were there. I have thus taken a lot of poetic license in presenting the accounts related in the Book.

A lot of the events concerning the young protagonist take place during the 1950s and many a chapter is devoted more to the *lifestyle* of the East African Asian than the protagonist's *life story*.

In the case of colonial Kenya and other such countries this is the period, I believe, more than any other in comparatively recent times, which appears shrouded in the mists of time and nostalgia due to a number of historical and other reasons invoking images of Jungle Safari Adventures, *The White Hunter*, *Tarzan the Ape Man* (the films were often shot in Kenya), The Mau Mau Rebellion and the then, Indian, colonial as well as African way of life.

Last but not least, the territories' raw, earthy and natural beauty, flora and fauna, some of which has now been lost to us.

A word about political correctness: Due to the time frame and setting of this book, the reader might find a disregard of the above. The colonial period as well as the language during school days of the times are the main cause and the writer has occasionally presented the language and style as it was in use at the time.

Introduction

Africa and Kenya, the coming of the Asian

Africa. In the old days and even until recent times it was referred to as the lost, the dark continent. Even today, there are some who are total strangers to this vast, beautiful part of the planet. For this reason, Asians who have not lived there are somehow alienated from those who have lived and loved the way of life that still exists, albeit with some restrictions. What follows is a hint of what one would expect in terms of natural beauty and its surroundings. Again, whilst mainly referring to Kenya, some descriptions could well apply to other parts of the continent.

Best appreciated in the rural areas, the rising sun at dawn over the Acacia trees, or the palms at the coast, the pink along with the blue, the dusk with the golden and purple skies, the migrating birds in varying profusion to nest, the heady smell of the earth, the orange coloured terrain, and the people. Of course, the people. The various tribes, Kikuyu, Luo, Maasai, Wakamba and the Giriama at the coast. Some more business-like in their approach than others, but on a personal level extremely friendly and despite hardships, laughing away their blues come what may. Black is even more beautiful here, with their wide smiles displaying perfectly symmetrical teeth, filed to perfection according to tribal customs. The Maasai with their bodies painted with red earth, spears in hand, donning lions' manes which cover their heads. Their dances, a must for the appreciating tourist and tribal customs as in the case of the Maasai killing a lion to prove manhood.

The flora and fauna are some of the most varied on the planet. The majestic African Elephant, king of the jungle lion, the fastest land animal cheetah, the uniquely patterned giraffe, hippo, black and white rhinoceros, crocodile, baboon and various deer abounding in the forests.

With conservation and tourism very much a priority these are protected in the various game parks, although poaching, which was intermittently rampant in the earlier days remains a problem today for the game departments.

The flora include the rose and primrose from England, various lilies, including the Kenya national emblem the gloriosa, bougainvilleas, hibiscus (origin America) and others detailed later.

Butterflies and birds in endless variety and hues.

Among those which would count as wonders of the world are the countless pink flamingos at lake Nakuru and seeing them rise in the equally pink sky of the dawn, the amazing Rift Valley, the velvet dark skies with a million stars over tropical nights, with the sound of crickets in grass and the often soundless forests with only the occasional rustle of leaves.

The ivory white coastline, again, is regarded as one of the best on the planet. The interior teeming with tropical fruit and vegetables, as are the numerous flowering plants in a land where anything and everything grows effortlessly.

Finally, the lakes, rivers and mountains would complete the picture with Mount Kenya at approximately 17,000 feet being the second highest mountain in Africa (Mount Kilimanjaro in Tanzania at 19,028 feet is the highest). Lake Victoria, shared by all three territories and the river Nile which, like the vast Rift Valley, ranges from eastern Africa to Egypt in the north and flows through part of the three territories.

Kenya was very much a jewel in the colonial crown among its African territories.

In recent years, archaeological finds show the first human to have evolved there and as further proof of the theory that the earth was one big landmass, you find references to Eastern Africa and its wonders in Indian mythology, for example naming the Blue and White Nile as *Neel and Shwet Ganga* respectively and Mount Kilimanjaro as *mandar parvat.*

For most Asians, it was the idyllic lifestyle, socially home away from home, domestic help, near perfect climate and the best of all three worlds: their own, the Western – despite some restrictions until Independence – and the African.

Small wonder then, that once, having *lived* in (East) Africa, it becomes a part of you and your memories, a thousand miles away you may be, remaining with you, in your psyche, veins, and blood, many still conversing in the Swahili language with like-friends decades after their physical departure.* Conversely a part of you undoubtedly remains behind.

In many cases the original business names have been retained for the enterprises in the new countries of settlement.

Obviously, the elders reminisce the days much more, having lived practically their whole lives in those countries and their first social identity and inquiry to others on meeting for the first time is what part of East Africa the other hails from and they invariably find there is always a social connection somewhere!!

Chances are an hour later you will still find them, in animated conversation, reliving the old days ...

---

* The expression *bana* (*bwana*) meaning sir or boss is used in nearly every conversation by East Africans

Arrival of the Indian from the sub-continent

Travel for trade had been going on for centuries from the sub-continent to East Africa in the early boats/dhows. The first migrations for settlement took place in the late nineteenth century by renowned tradesmen such as Alidina Visram and subsequently thousands of workers were recruited from colonial India to build the Kenya Uganda Railway, a British government project, in order to link the uncultivated interior with the coast for trade and travel. There was initially a lot of opposition to the construction as the British tax payer had to fund the project, purely for expansion of the British empire and it was at one stage referred to as the 'Lunatic line!':

What it will cost no one can express
What is its subject no brain can suppose
Where it will start from no one can guess
Where it will end up nobody knows
Where it is going no one can define
It clearly is nought but a lunatic line!
(source: the weekly journal *Truth*)

Despite this seemingly crazy project and its undeniable difficulties, especially the almost impassable terrain, the project was finally completed in 1903 with some of the Indian workforce remaining behind.

Some cultivated land granted by the colonial government, others became small shopkeepers creating bazaars where Indian currency, law and customs prevailed.

Later, professionals too arrived and settled in the bigger centres like Mombasa, Kisumu and Nairobi ...

Chapter 1

Dadaji (Grandfather) arrives at Voi

Ram Vakil, Shekhar's grandfather worked in the Indian
civil service and when certain friends and acquaintances began applying to go across the seas to this new and
hopefully prosperous land of Eastern Africa he too applied successfully as a station master at one of the
railway outposts.

Voi is a small village/railway town, approximately a
hundred miles from the coast which is where Grandpa
or D*adaji* got posted. This was a couple of years before
the beginning of the Second World War.

Shekhar's father and Uncle were finishing college in
India and worked for a while, got married and only
came to the new continent with their young families a
couple of years after the war around the time of Indian
independence and as Dadaji was approaching retire-
ment.

'Station Master Vakil' as he was known, Dadaji was
both admired and feared by the few Indian families
residing at Voi as well as, and especially by, the native
African workers. A story went that whilst returning
from a neighbouring village, he and his trusted worker
were confronted by a group of hyenas and it was only
the former's die-hard courage which succeeded in chasing off the animals. From that day onwards, the station-
master was hailed as a hero amongst all the
station/village folk.

There were less complimentary stories as well, about
Dadaji's courage, when on one occasion Shekhar's

father and uncle (*Kakaji*) were visiting from India (still in their late teens), and one of them got into an argument with the elder, whereupon he was dragged into the bush and forced to spend the night there. Needless to say, the elder later repented and fetched his offspring back by the early hours of the morning.

He needn't have worried though, as there were trees which one could climb and hide in during the night and in any case a berserk Grandma (*Dadiji)* had secretly sent a manservant to look after the poor victim, along with a couple of other workers. However, had the Master caught wind of all this ...

As Dadaji used to recount to subsequent generations the railway enabled increase of trade and established far reaching contacts. The moment the sound of the train whistle was heard the village folk, all excited, rushed with tea, water and meals for the passengers turning the remote railway station into a social ground; news from other towns was exchanged and trade was discussed. The contribution of the Indian, residing in such isolated and harsh conditions, was in no small measure responsible for opening up the interior for trade and social progress and that too without any aid from the Government.

Chapter 2

Road to Mombasa
Life in Paradise. First Home. First School

When one approached the island of Mombasa, by road from Nairobi and upcountry, one was greeted with mixed sights, sounds and smells.

In the distance, as you descended the hilly motorway having passed the small townships of Changamwe, Mazeras, Miritini and Mariakani, on the outskirts you see the Kilindini Harbour emerging from a narrow strip of land before joining the Indian Ocean. The distant sea air is mixed with a few unsavoury scents as waste units and other not so pleasant sites are located here. Perhaps it is the proverbial compost and flower – rose and thorn – paradox, for once having passed this and the township, you saw the coastal beauty in all its glory, with tall palm trees and their huge fan-like leaves, already seen earlier, getting more profuse, with soft breezes in tandem moving through large mango groves, cashew and almond trees and other tropical vegetation, with the roads getting sandier as you approach the town itself.

You drove through the central locality and if, like many ex-inhabitants, you happened to be returning after a substantial spell of absence, you would remember Rip van Winkle and how he felt after his decades of sleep in the children's story you read in your childhood.

You would not have been blamed for the feeling. The central township seemed to remain in a time warp with *Makupa* Road and *Mnazi Moja, Salim, Makadara and*

Kilindini Roads having changed little. Those two and three storey residences with the names of the elder son of the Indian family engraved at the time of construction (*Ashok Nivas, 1953*) remained as they were, albeit refurbished periodically.

In more recent times, however, the urban landscape has changed as new housing and modernisation has taken place.

You would see the ubiquitous Arab traders selling *kahawa* (coffee) whilst clanging their porcelain mini-cups.

Likewise, African vendors with their fruit and vegetables – especially mango and fresh coconut and others with their 'repertoire' of a hundred different merchandises ranging from car spares to clothing – *kitenge* (African patterned) shirts and Nike shoes to local beer!

Moving in

After their arrival from the sub-continent and brief stay at Voi, the family moved to the coastal town of Mombasa. The joint family (a system which is still prevalent among Asian families) comprised Grandfather, Grandma, Shekhar's uncle, being the elder brother Prafulchandra (*Kakaji*), tall and slim, sporting a moustache, easy going in nature and often spoiling the kids, wife Bhanumati (*Kakiji*), a rare graduate for an Asian lady of her age group in those days and a teacher with an austere nature, son Nilesh and his twin sisters, Radha and Reshma younger by a few years. Next came Shekhar's father Dineshchandra, sober, bespectacled with a hair parting in the middle, as men occasionally did in those days and very much looking the part of a *vakil* (lawyer), and Shekhar's mother Shantaben, again in tune with her name, a quiet and demure housewife,

Shekhar and his sister Geeta who was a couple of years younger than him.

As for the children's nature, Nilesh somehow went after his uncle, studious, cool and collective whereas Shekhar turned out to be very much an all-rounder, inheriting a hint of the uncle's mischief-making and auntie's artistry. As the years went by, he showed a love for drama, cricket and a general appreciation of the arts and mummy's loving nature for any and all.

As for the girls, Geeta was reserved, studious but nevertheless friendly when circumstances demanded it. The twins, pretty, lovable and ever smiling were spoiled by all from the word go and were thus a handful.

They all arrived from Voi with an Indian trader, who roamed the land in his twin Ford station wagons ('Box bodies' they were sometimes called). It was a dusty and hot journey as the roads in those days were not tarmacked.

The War had been over for a few years and the new decade of the '50s was anticipated. Kenya too had been affected by the conflict and the end of the war had brought optimism and a euphoric feeling in the hearts of the people.

Originally Mombasa was the capital, being the only developed area. From 1907 onwards Nairobi became the seat of power, due to interior development brought about by the railway, as well as the fertile highlands and cooler climate, thus there were considerably fewer white colonial administrators at the coast.

The first home was a rented property in 'old town'; so called 'old', because this is where the first Portuguese invaders arrived after the famous sailor Vasco Da Gama landed en route during his sea voyage to the east in 1498. After the departure of the Portuguese it was the Arabs who settled.

In the past, when you walked through the narrow streets and bazaars of the old town, you could easily be forgiven for mistaking it for a street in Lisbon or a Middle Eastern town, in the event you had happened to visit these. (This too, in recent times has changed for a newer outlook). The house where the family would put up was one of a group of spacious, though basic dwellings, and was located off the main road, which led through narrow streets, small Arab houses on either side, to the prominent Salim Road, housing the main *sokoni* (market), offices and shops.

The best thing most of the family members, especially the children, liked about it was that it was only approximately 40 yards from the sea-front although there was no beach or swimming facilities. At the edge of the sea-front you had protective metal bars (of a sort) for children and steps on the right leading down to a Yachting Marina Club. The view across the water, however could rival any picture post-card. Dhows and various boats with sails at full mast passing by, with, on the far left, the famous Nyali Bridge joining the island with the north, which would take you to the beaches and hotels that had slowly started springing up, and beyond to the smaller coastal towns of Malindi and Lamu. On the far opposite you could see the bungalows with brick rooftops lined in neat rows among the palms and other vegetation, obviously belonging to the more affluent, mostly colonial population.

The house itself, its stone walls painted in white brilliance, was spacious enough to accommodate the three-generation joint family.

Although there was complaint of not enough sunlight at times, it was apparently so designed to keep cool in the hot climate at the coast. The sticky heat meant you could do with two, even three showers a day, one around each mealtime at least for those at home! Grandpa was given the best room, one with the sea-face and here he rocked in his rocking chair regaling the grandchildren with his stories, amidst taking in the fresh sea air in gulps along with his Yogic breathing. The upstairs terrace was filled with large stone pots and tubs, which was one of grandma and mother's departments and they grew *tulsi* (basil) and other plants. The back garden, though small, boasted a papaya and guava tree, the fruits of which the kids fought over.

The older boys, Nilesh and Shekhar were six to seven years old and joined nursery school where they learned English and vernacular alphabets, basic sums, a bit about punch-ups and of course, hating girls! Not that they were tops in the last two categories, since a particular boy – call him Salil – turned bad behaviour into a fine art. Not only did he steal or grab sweets from every girl possible, at home time he performed his kick routine every few days. As he descended the school steps, he, for reasons best known to him alone, kicked each unsuspecting boy available at the Achille's Tendon resulting in standing boys rolling down the steps and those sitting cowering, all in tears.

Whether it was inspiration from the early, black and white Roy Rogers' Westerns so popular at the time or just the first inklings of juvenile heroism, Shekhar somehow managed to gather a couple of his mates, who had been, at one time or the other, victims of this comparatively huge boy.

'This has got to stop, and straight away,' said our hero to his friends. 'His parents collect him at 4.00 sharp in the evening. That gives us half an hour. I'm going to lure him to the back of the caretaker's place and then it's him and us. So, one fine Thursday afternoon that's just what happened. After a bloody but enjoyable behind the school romp three against one the mates managed to make him see the error of his ways.

Even Mrs Shah, the Assistant Head who had been unable to tame this 'star of the school' gave a knowing nod and did not delve much into the incident, despite a parental complaint.

A hint of the distant past ...

Not far from the Vakil abode was the famous monument of Fort Jesus built in 1594, a testament to invasions by the Portuguese. Indian masons took part in the construction and one can see their craftsmanship apparent as it does in many Indian Forts on the sub-continent. The Portuguese unlike the Omani and Mazrui Arabs came, plundered and left Mombasa successively beginning with Vasco Da Gama in 1498. Despite their non-settlement, as they visited the island for a good part of two centuries, they left their influence in the architecture which is clearly evident in the housing as one moves through the old town. The Arabs in contrast made settlements, inter married, took many of the locals away as slaves and converted the natives to Islam. Thus, Arabic influence in the architecture as well as the language and people is much more profound.

Mombasa, unlike the interior cities which came into prominence after the construction of the railway, thus has a surprisingly long history due to its coastal location.

It was known to sailors and adventurers as early as the first century A.D. An unknown Greek describing it in his anonymous account Periplus as *Tonike*.

Once named East Africa's 'Queen among Cities', Mombasa is also referred to in the epic poem by John Milton, *Paradise Lost*, thus:

'The Empire of Negus to his utmost port,
Ercoco and the less maritime Kings

Mombaza and Quiloa and Melind (Malindi).'

Earlier the island has been visited for trade by Indians and the Chinese who exchanged silk, printed cottons and spices in return for gold and ivory.

The invasions by the Portuguese and the Arabs continued until the 1880s, when Kenya finally came under British protection ...

The best years of our lives ...

Father and *Kakaji* joined up with a reputable law firm in town. *Kakiji* was one of the few Indian women of her generation who had graduated and she taught in a primary school – and a tough teacher she was too, as the children learned from their older friends.

In the evenings, like most 'Mombasians' it was the Light House, *the* meeting place. Walks in the evening, cool sea-breezes, mogo (cassava) and makai (corn on the cob) roasted by the vendors in the open and fresh coconut-water, each age and social group chatting away, armchairs and radio music as spool tapes were yet to come, the south coast opposite, accessible by ferry leading to Tanganyika and the remains of that old ship sunk years ago, bobbing away in the distance. Nor was it over as it turned dark, the moon and the stars gazing down, envious of the humans below who wouldn't have exchanged it for the world! Of course, for the kids it was fun time at that age anyway, however the grown-ups talked about it for years afterwards – as the surviving ones do today – that these were indeed 'The best years of our lives.'

The entire life-style so accommodating, almost idyllic, for all. For the menfolk lunch-breaks at noon meant being home for lunch, followed by siesta, a few hours back to work and then off to the Light House.

Like most tropical or developing countries, for the women folk home help and servants were the norm, making it a comfortable life as most did not work.

Chapter 3

Ali, the first *mwalimu* (teacher): The early years

One of the first requirements for the family, upon arrival at Mombasa had been for the elders to set about hiring domestic help, with the assistance of friends or neighbours.

Ali turned up one morning along with the house worker of a neighbour. Well-built and with a friendly and polite disposition, a light beard adding to his maturity, he managed to impress everyone from the outset. The elders reckoned he was in his late 30s. After the customary *Jambo*(s) (hello, greetings) he inquired in detail his duties, hours of work and the salary. When asked about previous references, he replied, 'I have worked for a *mzungu* bachelor gentleman at the other end of town, performing housework, tending the garden and also cooking for my employer. He has moved upcountry and Syed here who is from my hometown in Malindi said a job was available.'

Becoming everyone's favourite for various reasons, he was indispensable after a while. The mums could not manage without his shopping help, assisting in the kitchen – especially as *Kakiji* was away during the day, teaching. Likewise the menfolk came to rely on his immaculate laundering for their wardrobe. As time went by he displayed the many other skills he had up his sleeve.

The twin girls were just toddlers when Ali had appeared on the scene and it was he who helped feed and put them to bed at night mostly, singing lullabies in Swahili and sometimes even picking up Indian ones, in broken Hindi and Gujarati from the mums to the gentle sways of the string-pulling of the Indian crib. As the senior cousins grew up, the man took them to the near-by play nursery and later to primary or first school, in the family-driven saloon and returned doing the shopping for the kitchen or other such tasks.

An exceedingly fast worker, he always had some time on his hands, before retiring for the evening to his quarters or going out as, per the custom, his family was back at the village/home town which he would visit from time to time.

Thus when the older boys returned from school Ali was waiting with his own brand of tuition.

'*Fanya haraka, badirisha nguo*' (hurry up, change your clothes), he would command.

'First, we shall go to the park, practise our football and running, and if you do well, I'll tell you a story or two. They spent almost an hour at the nearby public gardens and Fort Jesus which had cannons both outside as well as inside. The boys particularly loved to pretend manning the ones inside the Fort which faced the Indian Ocean as lookout weaponry. After progressing from these, they learned three and then two-wheel cycling.

Ali regaled them with stories of Kenya both past and present. 'Years and years ago, this country and Mombasa especially was run by the native Africans, by tribes such as the Giriama, the Swahili and the Ndorobo. Then came the Zenj people from Azania, Omani and then Mazrui Arabs followed, finally came the Portuguese. They all fought each other and took the original natives as slaves. Some stayed and inter-married with the locals, converting them to Islam. That is why you can see black people having Islamic/Arabic names.'

As the years progressed, Ali used to talk about life and

matters in general; considering his limited education he surprised the elders at times, who came to entrust the children fully to him.

One fine day Shekhar, now about seven or eight, proclaimed, 'Ali, henceforth I'm going to call you *Mwalimu*. I think I've learned more from you than the school teachers.'

Ali laughed his gruff, hearty laugh and asked, 'What special name shall I give **you** then? I know, I'll call you *Kumar*,' this being a popular Indian title given to young people. It has also invariably been a favourite (part) pseudonym/title among Indian Film stars which is where Ali obviously picked it up, as everybody watched Indian films. Over the years, however there were quite a few alternatives added. Sometimes it was Roy Roja (Rogers) after the screen/comic book cowboy or Tarzan or simply *Kijana* (youngster).

Their friendship evolved over the years despite the age difference and Ali became a friend, philosopher and guide to the youngster ...

Chapter 4

Saturday at the *Sokoni* (Market)

'Dineshchandra (Shekhar's dad) even in those early days had employed a part-time driver or chauffeur to take the family around. Esmail was a safe and superb driver. He had worked with transport companies and taxi firms for years, having driven the length and breadth of Kenya over a long period. When the family or men folk, while on business, made occasional trips to the upcountry, capital Nairobi or beyond, Esmail was their man.

It was Esmail who drove the mums each Saturday to the *sokoni* for their weekly purchases. When the ladies went shopping, elder cousin Naresh and Shekhar were left in charge of their younger siblings. They thought they were doing the job pretty well, what with Ali around, doing his chores in and out of the house. However, one Saturday Ali got tied up with something, and left to themselves the boys invited their entire 'neighbourhood gang' home. 'The mums are not due back for a couple of hours, and Ali has got an urgent errand, so let's make the most of it,' they said. The offer was too tempting to refuse and so the brood arrived in no time. They raided – and messed up – the kitchen and then turned the living room – despite its limited size – and the rear veranda into a playground. Some played with the 'Noddy' and 'Goofy' cars that *Dadaji* and *Ba* had bought for the kids' birthdays. Others jumped over sofas, one turned on the phonograph with whatever vinyl 78rpm was available and yet another rode on the sisters' tricycle. Their only Sikh/Punjabi friend, Sukhbir, was just attempting a somersault in the hallway, having adjusted his head gear, when the front door was almost kicked open and lo and behold, who else but *Kakiji* made entry, her hands full of shopping, hence the push with the foot. Apparently, the ladies had finished their shopping early this Saturday. For a few seconds, she just stood there, her normally semi-austere features hardening by the second, her mouth half-ajar at the spectacle which beheld her!

Shekhar's mum and Esmail with heavier goods were following behind, the former unaware of what was to come, was rambling away, half to herself, about the shopping and food prices, 'Things have become so expensive, one wonders where they'll stop ... but what can one do, one has to eat ...'

Some of the kids in the living room froze at the sight of the adults but the rest, elsewhere, carried on with their hullabaloo unaware until their 'hosts' had to inform them that the party was over.

Finally, *Kakiji* began rattling her keys, and the slice-through-the-air silence meant this was all you could hear. The 'guests' all filed past and out into the street sunshine without a word. The clean-up took a good hour which of course, the boys carried out gladly, simultaneously wondering what other punishment was in store. They did not have long to wait. After tea, the adults summoned the senior boys and delivered their verdict, 'Well, you've all had a great morning, we can see,' said the elder of the two, 'poor Ali had this delivery to make and you boys obviously thought nobody was going to return for a while. Well, so that you are not tempted again, we have decided that the two elder boys, shall accompany us each Saturday morning to the *Sokoni!*' The boys opened their mouths in protest but no words emanated as the elder continued, 'There shall be no further discussion on the subject.'

Angry and speechless initially, after the first week, the guilt bearers began to enjoy their Saturday outings.

The first visit:
the sights ... the sounds ... the smells ...

The main market was off Salim Road one of the prominent business areas. Traders had their various stalls and the variety of fresh produce was abundant. Vegetables, fresh as well as dry fruit in one section and clothing and other merchandise in a separate area.

The noise on Saturday morning was deafening, cars and other vehicles blasting away with their horns, the bicycles' bells ringing away, dogs yelping, chickens clucking whether in their baskets or on human shoulders, three at a time and held by their legs. Human chatter in Arabic, Swahili, Indian and occasional English, including ones by the native women carrying the *bhoga khikhapu* (matted baskets) carrying vegetables, supported by the straps on their near-bald heads. If they didn't get you here at the *sokoni* you could rest assure they would finally find their way sooner or later to your residence announcing themselves with something like '*mama, bhoga ... viazi, matara ...*'

The sweet smell of fresh mango and other *matunda* (fruit), and in contrast the not so fresh smell of discarded or rotten fruit and vegetable plus thankfully at a distance the smell of fish and meat often stale. Being the coast, the ubiquitous sound of *kahawa* (coffee) cups, and the oily smell wafting from the adjoining gulley locating Indian hotels, frying *bhajias* and similar savouries ...

Perhaps the boys were not wrong in calling it what they did, the green market, for, besides the mostly green produce, you not only had green canvas for roof cover but also the trellis-like green matting as side barriers. On the first day, the inquisitive juniors naughtily began peeping through these, before being pulled away by the elders. The fruit section reluctantly became the boys' favourite – since there were no sweets available. Some in huge triangular mounds (guavas), others boxed (mangoes, pineapples and cashew fruits) ...

The boys hitherto had never been fans, however it was in these markets that they became aware that there was a tasty and healthy alternative to sweets, for a while at least, especially when *Auntiji* in one of her lighter moods decided to give a scientific lecture on the virtues of fruit consumption! 'I know you boys would prefer eating your (unripe) mangoes and guavas (green often with red flesh and yellow with the cream one) by the roadside,' meaning the street vendors who sold their fruits the yummy way, chopped horizontal from the top and then sliced vertical, hexagonally and dipped in salt and red chilli! 'however once in a while try them all on their own. One of the reasons our ancestors lived a long and healthy life was due to having a large proportion of fruit in their diet,' she encouraged.

Among the fruits were mangoes of the coast, which went all over the country and exported abroad, even today and the adults never tired of extolling the virtues of the Lamu mangoes which grew at the small northern port. Long, curved and yellow, they taste as lovely as they are in appearance. There are the purple berries, sweet and sour (*jamuda* in Indian) named obviously after their colour. Date and cashew fruit are also a coast speciality. Many an afternoon was spent after school with boys' catapults firing away obtaining the exquisite almond fruit and others, the former often staining their white shirts and their mouths with the red juice. The giant green coconuts were of course left to the experts who deftly climbed the tall palms. The papaya and banana almost grew wild and in one's backyard and all one needed was to prod them with a long stick when ripe, provided you were not preceded by a rival!

Insofar as the boys' punishment was concerned, the first few Saturdays went fine but then the novelty began to wear off, and in any case fruit and veg still only came second best to sweets and ice-cream!

Finally, one fine Saturday a decision was made to protest, and upon arrival, a couple of fruit mounds were 'accidentally' toppled. The vendors chased, shouting *watoto mbaya, choonga watoto* (bad children, look after the children), as the latter attempted to escape their wrath. The elders were taken aback, both angry and embarrassed. Apologies were offered and thereafter Esmail was in charge of one quarry and the ladies, the other.

By now, fortunately for the boys, the year was coming to a close and in the new school year, as more mature activities like tennis ball cricket were taken up, the youngsters were finally released from their punishment.

Chapter 5

On Ghosts ... and Graveyards

By the time he was about seven, Shekhar had acquired a fondness for all sorts of reading, and like many boys his age this included ghost tales and a fascination for ghosts. He often wondered what it would be like to confront such a creature.

There was an Arab boy living nearby, who often came to see the cousins play, and always watched from a distance. Shekhar's cousin Suresh, a few years older, who lived in town came for a visit one weekend and the boys were playing by the sea front. The Arab boy – who later introduced himself as Abdul – ventured into juvenile conversation and after a while suddenly asked '*una taka ku ona uchawe?*' (would you like to see a witch?) The boys looked at each other in amazement at the question.

They asked in Swahili, 'How do you propose to provide us with one?' and the boy replied, 'I will take you to the *Kabristan* (Islamic Graveyard) at the other end of town. That is where she resides.'

The boys agreed shakily and Abdul said he would call the next day.

Most of the adults were attending a function that evening. Towards dusk, their friend knocked at the boys' window. Shekhar was initially in two minds but the presence of his elder cousin who was his *Guru, Ustad,* Hero, whatever you may wish to call him, raised his spirits and although Suresh would clearly have preferred someone older, he was pestered into allowing his protégé to come along. 'You know I won't get a chance like this again,' pleaded Shekhar as if it was a once in a lifetime, special opportunity!

It was fairly dark when they finally arrived at their destination. Their 'Guide' had borrowed a small torch, and they were led in by the apparently, experienced visitor! (He proudly informed them he had come here with his friends twice before!)

They saw graves with Islamic plaques and inscriptions on them, wreaths lying on the *mazaar/kabar* (grave). It was luckily a full moon night, but the moon kept disappearing into the clouds. Owls hooted softly and they had initially seen kites circling above them but upon arrival this had ceased, the birds obviously having nested.

Their peculiar shrill, trailing cries were heard all day at the coast in specific areas, the birds invariably flying in circular motion. Crickets cried in sporadic pockets of grass and there were a few trees at the far end. They sighted the caretaker's dwelling and quite a distance away, a hut, where, their host pointed out, lived Fatima.

The boys had heard of 'Witch' Fatima who lived at the *Kabristan*, according to the lucky few who claimed to have seen her. Despite the presence of a caretaker, she insisted on staying in her little hut. She had apparently lost her husband and children in some tragedy and after their burial, refused to move from the site, making it her makeshift home. Although few had seen her in recent times Abdul assured the boys she was around, mentioning his two previous visits and having sighted her, albeit from a safe distance. 'Brace yourselves as true *dumey* (He-men),' said their host, 'she is known to self-converse, along with hoots of laughter in between, which can be most intimidating.'

They suddenly heard sounds and voices. Three men carrying some object were making for the end of the yard. The youngsters lay down behind the plaques, horizontally. The moon, due to the hazy sky appeared briefly. Shekhar, with typical juvenile curiosity, looked up to his Cousin and opened his mouth to whisper the obvious, but his elder hushed him up with his hands. Apparently, the best place to hide what appeared to be a thief's booty was the graveyard, as nobody in their right mind would search there!

The men dug beneath a tree, hid what appeared to be a box and left, looking hither and thither ... They would discuss this later, as Abdul was guiding them towards the hut. Everything was absolutely quiet as the earlier sounds seemed distant. Before they could peek in, from behind their backs, suddenly came a shriek of laughter, a kind Shekhar had never before heard. A ghost-like woman appeared before them as they turned around in fear. Tall and thin as a rake, her dress totally ragged, hair unkempt and in dishevelled fashion. In the sparse moonlight the boys saw her grey, bloodshot eyes and finally her long, slender hands, fingers supporting her equally long nails, her teeth a dentist's nightmare, not that there would ever have been an encounter between the two!

For a moment, the youngest of the heroes thought the woman would grab one of them. *'Watoto! Watoto mchanja! Una fanya je' (nini), hapo saa hi?'* (Children! Naughty children! What are you doing here at this hour?) She looked straight into each of their eyes in turn, half-smiling, half-intimidating. Shekhar felt as if a slab of ice had been placed on his young, delicate shoulders, feeling his body nerves would suddenly pop out and curl at their ends. Never in his brief stay on earth until this moment, he thought to himself, had he encountered such fear. Shaking, each of them clasping the hand of the next, they dared not look at each other. With hair on edge, the youngest whispered to his elder,

'I think I'm going to wee wee myself.' Big Brother Suresh tightened his hand grip, suggesting control. Young Abdul in reply to the lady's poser ventured, '*sisi sisi*,' (we, we or us, us) but could not say further, possibly because, obviously not having seen the woman at this close a range on his previous visits, he was also in a 'wee wee' situation. Of course, the double entendre/ pun/quip would not have occurred to any of them at the time, as Shekhar kept asking himself what on earth he was doing in this place and what the family would think of it all ... when and if they found out ... and most importantly if ... they ever got out alive from this god forsaken place ...

Their torturer kept on with her ramblings, laughing intermittently, for a good ten to fifteen minutes. Their abjection came to an end when the woman briefly, turned sideways distracted by an owl hoot as well as some godly animal force rustling among the sparse vegetation around. '*Kimbiya! Sasa!*' (run! now!) cried Abdul, seizing the opportunity. Clenching their fists, they used all their reserves and rushed for the gates. It was slightly downhill on the way out. The younger members fell twice, but the bleeding or bruised knees were a mild punishment compared to what they had just endured. The relief that each yard further brought was ecstasy and no one looked back once, sweat dripping from all pores.

In a few minutes, they were on Salim Road, the bright lights a heavenly contrast to that long stretch of darkness they had suffered. They rushed down towards old Mombasa, avoiding the occasional gazes of adults who wondered what the urchins, especially the state they were in, had been up to, at this time. As they approached home, nothing was discussed; they hastily said goodbye to their mate, and barely managed to pacify their elderly and sole adult in charge that evening.

Needless to say, the boys could barely sleep and for several subsequent nights; the image of that creature, who or whatever it was, came to haunt them repeatedly. The conversation each night, in whispers of course, was the same:

Shekhar: Suresh *Bhai*, are you asleep? I can't get to sleep. I don't ever want to see that Abdul again. What were those three men doing? What do you think happened to that box they were hiding? And ... and ... that Fatima ...

Suresh: Shekhar, for God's sake shut up. And as for your questions, the answer is I don't know and don't want to know. GO TO SLEEP!

As the days went by, however, the boys seemed to come through it all as peaceful sleep finally returned to them.

Or so they thought ...

A fortnight or so later, they were playing marbles by the sea-front when cousin Suresh happened to mention their adventure, since that is how they now referred to it, to one of their older playmates. To their utter shock and amazement, the youngster burst out laughing, and carried on doing so derogatively. When he finally stopped, he stared at the cousins: 'Don't give me that rubbish! Old Fatima?! Why, everyone knows she's been dead for over a year!'

Chapter 6

Moving out

The joint family moved a year later into a comparatively newer part of town, *Mnazi Moja* (literally, single coconut) and *Ganjoni*. This was also rental accommodation, which they put up with for nearly a year, before the adults got tired of paying rent and landlords, especially Mr Patel at this house, who turned up on the 29th of every month with a sheepish smile on his face for collection.

Driving urges

When the family moved uptown for a year in the house owned by Mr Patel, there was need for further domestic help. The house was slightly larger with a fair-sized garden and the smaller car was changed for a black Wolseley, purchased nearly new, which Dad rewarded himself with, when they expanded their law practice. *Kakaji* rarely drove his vintage 1937 Ford Prefect, so he left all such matters to his younger brother.

The additional domestic need was satisfied by the arrival of young Osman, Ali's nephew. 'This is Osman, my nephew who will be assisting me,' introduced Ali one morning. The new arrival was tall, with a boyish, almost cheeky smile and of slim build. 'He has worked for a couple of families and also been a shop assistant with a prominent Arab in old Mombasa. His domestic specialities include gardening, perfect ironing – which he will take over from me – and spotless cleaning; when he starts polishing something, he has to be dragged away from his quarry at times!' laughed Ali.

Osman became Dad's favourite, due to his spotless maintenance of the car, in and out and perfect ironing, whereby he even surpassed the previous efforts of his Uncle. He was cheekily shy at first, but then opened up to the family members, entertaining the children and Shekhar's Mum with his own versions of Indian film numbers. Thus, for example:

Gore gore o banke chhore became *chori chori babaki chori* and

Lapak jhapak tu aa re badariya became *chapati chapati tu aa re ...* *

He was expert at many forms of dance and this included Master Bhagwan's *Albela* (film) routines, which most Africans had taken to in a big way, both in the cinema aisles as well as in homes or streets!

One hot Saturday, while most of the children were still asleep and the men were preparing to go to the office, it went quiet all of a sudden. Normally one would hear conversation amidst the low-key singing between the workers and ladies, now there was none. So Father looked down to the street where Osman was supposed to be cleaning the car. All hell broke loose as there was no sign of the car or the young worker.

'Ali, Shanta, *Motabhai*,' shouted Dad. Normally quite cool of demeanour, this was one of his rare outbursts. 'The car's gone and no sign of Osman either.'

Ali rushed out of the kitchen along with Shekhar's mum. Expressed the embarrassed worker, 'Now I know why the fellow had been asking me all sorts of questions

---

* English translation 'O fair, handsome young man' changed to a version that only young Osman understood
'Rain clouds come forth' - the young man's silly version says 'chapati (Indian bread) come forth'.

about the car the last few days including the driving manoeuvres. It looks as if he could not control himself and has made off on a joy ride.'

The children had got up by now and found the whole situation quite amusing, not realising the possible serious consequences. *Kakaji* said, 'It's no point at this stage informing the police, as Ali is pretty sure the young man should return soon.'

'That is, if he doesn't knock someone first or someone him,' said Dad, looking understandably concerned.

'What if he's driven off to Malindi or somewhere?' said Geeta, trying to be helpful.

'That's all we need,' sighed Dad.

'Hush,' said *Kakiji* to the children, 'go back to your rooms.'

Prafulbhai (*Kakaji*) amidst the seriousness of it all, could not help smirking slightly.

'I'm sorry, I fail to see the humour,' said Dad, dryly. After all it was his car, and purchased nearly new so recently.

The ladies calmed their men. 'Just wait and see for a couple of hours; we could then inform the police.'

In the event, it was the police that came to inform the family at around half past eleven, almost three hours after the discovery. A most austere-looking *wazungu* police constable along with his native *Askari* (native policeman) rang the bell and presently walked in followed by a sheepish, handcuffed Omar. Advised the constable: 'This young chap was found driving without a license and I'm pretty sure, the owner's permission, on the outskirts, at Nyali. We had a couple of phone complaints, as he had been doing almost 50mph when we gave chase and got him!'

The policeman waited for a response.

After a long hard look at the 'defendant', Father, in his usual professional manner, advised he wasn't pressing any charges and that the young man was in his employment.

'Well, Sir, I'd keep an eye on him henceforth, if I were you.' So saying, the apprehender and his sidekick departed.

There was a long discussion between the menfolk – all four – and finally the wronged party thawed a little, and everybody even saw the humorous side to the situation, all except Osman since one could hear Dad, Uncle and Ali guffawing for quite a while amidst speculations on what must have been and what might have, but luckily did not.

Finally, Dad sombrely clinked the keys at Osman, meaning, 'No more keys for you.' The quality of his house work meant he was forgiven for this, his first 'crime,' but one thing was certain; the young driving enthusiast did not sit behind the wheel for a long, long time ...

Chapter 7

Sundays, seaside, cinema

The Sunday morning sky was splashed with strokes of flaming red, interspread with lavender and pink against a blue canvas. There wasn't a cloud visible, the temperature was comfortably warm as it was still mid-morning as the family made for Bamburi, the most popular of the beaches at Nyali among the Indian community.

The kids wanted to laze about in the hours of the morn, but as soon as Dad announced, 'Who's for Bambu-ri? Raise your hands,' there was no waiting. A brief bath, as there would be lots of swimming later on, a quick breakfast and everyone was ready. This was the favourite picnic site as far as the sea-side was concerned. Swimming in the sea, walking and playing in the sand – the whitest sand you could ever find on any beach on the planet many people claim – shell hunting, sand baskets for the kiddies and cooking *khichdi* on the open fire.

As many as six adults including close family friend K.K. Desai with their offspring on some of their laps were packed in Dad's Wolseley. How they managed to escape the traffic police, not to speak of the human burden on the vehicle, was anybody's guess. Upon arrival, everyone cooled off including the mums.

'Conservatism and modesty are not going to allow us to get into swimsuits,' said *Kakiji*, as they moved away from the menfolk slightly and splashed about amidst the warm turquoise waters, in their old *saris,* 'but we're going to have fun as much as the rest.'

Dad's closest friend K.K. Desai who loved to paint in his spare time, had his gear all ready. As he began his brush strokes, he spoke to his friend in artistic terms, 'Just look at those palms, Dineshchandra, tall and swaying in the breeze, with the fronds hitting against the long slender trunks, rather like tall, elegant maidens, with their long hair flowing and hitting gently against their lean forms, wouldn't you agree?'

'Well I suppose so, if you put it that way,' replied his more ascetic than artistic friend, who was less inclined to such things.

Grandpa, well into his healthy 80s was in his sand *Samadhi or* yogic trance with three fourths of his body buried in sand. 'Stop pestering *Dadaji* with your endless questions and go back to your sand baskets and shells,' chided the mums. The kids looked on in wonder and their questions did not exactly lack variety: 'How did you manage to go in there, *Dadaji*? How will you get out? Doesn't the sand itch? Won't the crabs bite?'

All that swimming and other activity worked up an appetite and after lunch and a short siesta on the arm chairs – for those who wanted it – the entourage made its way back by early afternoon which had to be spent recuperating, for more was to come in the evening. To be precise the 6 p.m. family picture show.

At around 4 p.m. the hustle and bustle started. 'Shanta, let's have some tea,' reminded Dad. 'I think I'll wear the pink one today,' said Shekhar's Mum, referring to her sari attire for the evening, while the primus stove was on, in the days before gas and electricity cooking. They discussed the forthcoming evening's entertainment, 'Haven't seen Ashok Kumar and Meena Kumari on screen in a long time,' said *Bhanukaki.* Film matters was one area where she seemed to let loose her otherwise uptight demeanour. She also loved and occasionally hummed the song numbers.

'Now's the time to ask *Kakiji* for some pocket money, before she becomes her *usual* self,' Shekhar and Nilesh would say to each other and grab the opportunity.

The Indian films, in those monochrome days, were love stories cum social dramas, many of them dealing with relevant issues, along with a lot of sentimentality, but the real highlights of course were the seven song numbers. Drenched in melody, often displaying hints of the light classical, with acknowledged vocalists, lyricists and composers, films often ran on the sheer strength of their musical scores. Advance bookings were usually avoided as the gregarious Indian guest had the habit of dropping in without pre-arrangement! It was the husband who queued endlessly at the box office, of course and even purchased tickets on the black market, as the alternative prospects of going back without being 'entertained' were frightening, to say the least!

After the show, 'Ice cream anyone?' for the kiddies and the *madafus* (coconut), the ubiquitous thirst quencher for the elders, as the patrons often strolled back home in the relative cool of the tropical night, with stars above for company, humming the songs they had just witnessed their favourite 'stars'(!) lip synchronising on the screen.

Light House 'sessions'

The Mombasa Light House was the evening and weekend relaxation haunt of Asian families at twilight hours and beyond. On a particular Friday evening for example the family would all get into the car and drive towards the southern part of town, passing the ferry service which could take you to the south coast and then Tanganyika (Tanzania). The older boys would unload the deck chairs and cars were parked on the grass area. Towards the sea front vendors sold their 'goodies' roasting them in their small vessels over charcoal fires.

'Shekharbhai, can I have some *mogo* (cassava) please?' twin Radha would plead. '*Makaai* (corn on the cob) for me,' said Reshma her sister. 'I'll just have a *madafu*,' said Geeta. The vendors would spice the first two with lashings of salt, red chili powder and lemon juice. Yummy!

Most of the adults would be chatting away or taking walks, with the sea-breeze soothing away the day's sticky heat they had endured. The stars shone above, bright and bountiful almost covering the heavens, and as far as your eyes could gaze spool tape recorders and portable gramophones played Indian film melodies. The song numbers too, in those days seemed to be apt to the ambience:

'*Ye raat ye chaandni phir kahaan?*' ... (when again. this night, this moonlight?),

'*Ye vaada karo chand ke samney*' (make me this promise with the moon as my witness!),

'*Ye raat bheegi bheegi ye mast fizaaen*' (this damp, damp night, this intoxicating milieu)

Chapter 8

The first Sunday of the month
Matunda, Mapera and ... the full monty!

Living on the coast with a hot clime meant come Sunday, people rushed to the beaches to spend much of the day among the sand, waves and palms. However, for variety, if nothing else, one of these Sundays was spent at a different venue.

The Vakils and a few other families had decided that the first Sunday would be spent at the farm of a well-known Indian farmer Karsanbhai Patel. His farm was located en route upcountry and the capital, at Changamwe, which was a small railway station and farming and industrial area. Karsanbhai had received the farm from his late uncle which meant the family had owned it for decades; in fact since before the war. They farmed vegetables mostly, but certain varieties of fruit too, and these were popular to the Indian palate and dinner table.

These included *pattarvelias* a large, leaf vegetable that is normally prepared with gram flour and then steam cooked or/and shallow fried with spices. Others were the highly popular, *baingans* (aubergines), cucumbers, *karelas* (bitter gourd), various kinds of spinach and potatoes.

The special kinds of fruit which were grown in orchards at the rear of the farm, including both varieties of the African *matunda* (passion fruit), the sweet and sour purple textured *jamuda*, a particular favourite of the Asian family, guavas and of course the mango. A small amount of cashew farming – for export – was also done.

On one such Sunday, four carloads with families made their way to the Patel *shamba* (farm). The families comprised: the (Doctor) Shahs, the (K.K.) Desais and their special Parsee friends the engineers besides the Vakils. Mrs Patel was a very garrulous, welcoming lady and a charming hostess and had been waiting apparently, for a while.

The hosts did not have any offspring of their own, so they treated the farm workers and their brood as their own. Upon arrival Mrs Patel took the guest ladies with her, 'Welcome, Welcome, I was wondering why you had not arrived.'

Normally the families would arrive quite early before the coastal sun's relentless heat took effect but today, explained Doctor Shah's missus, 'Your Doctor Saab always gets interrupted at the most unwanted hours being a "family doctor"; a last-minute call could not be avoided.'

The hostess was speaking non-stop, talking about the recent crop harvests and what they would prepare for lunch that afternoon. The ladies would get into the mood as open air cooking is always a delight. Said the hostess, with affection which was not new to her frequent guests, 'My Juma (the foreman) has arranged via the workers all the veg and fruit picked and ready, early this morning. I remember last time you all came, the workers were running around up to the last minute, so I told them, "no repetition of the same this time, or else",' she burst into a sudden guffaw, at her related threat. Suddenly she exclaimed, 'Oh, silly me, all this can wait, please come in and freshen up first.'

The bungalow or farm house was medium sized, built in the middle of the farm and of complete stone structure with a substantial veranda at the rear which looked onto further farm land and the orchards. The guests freshened up and took their customary walk around the farm. The smaller children all rushed towards the fruit trees and Shekhar and the older boys as per custom had a game of cricket with a tennis ball and then went exploring for any new sights since they had last visited, as they had not been with the elders on their last couple of visits.

The mothers shouted, 'Don't go too far now,' as, beyond the orchards was no-man's/neighbour's land which, although fenced up had large shrub areas possibly home to undesirable creatures. You could see at a long distance, the Kilindini Harbour with the occasional ship arriving for dock or departing for its journey across the Indian Ocean. The gents relaxed at their favourite spot, beneath some trees, outside the veranda.

Mr Engineer remarked, 'The crop looks good this year, Karsanbhai, both veg and fruit.'

Their host looked pleased and responded, 'Yes, the aubergines have turned out particularly good after the poor show for the last couple of years.'

'Well, there is never any poor show as far as this part of your *shamba* is concerned,' smiled Mr Engineer pointing to the huge garden plants section, almost entirely made up of the ubiquitous Bougainvillea flowering plants. The most profuse were the reds and orange but various other shades in magenta, pink and white also abounded.

'Do you know,' posed Mr Engineer to his group, 'that the species originated way out in the Andes in South America?'

'And what about the French sounding name?' asked *Kakaji*.

'Yes, that was named after a 16th century French navigator. They initially, I believe, spread over the

Asian Tropical countries, including India and some parts of far East.'

'As far as Kenya is concerned,' continued the botany expert – Mr Engineer had a detailed comment/answer to every botanical question – being an obsessive gardener, 'it is our chief plant in nurseries and gardens, boasting an endless variety of colours besides the main ones you see here.'

The gents had a long walk round the farm, presumably and not least, to whet their appetites and then settled down to a game of bridge, which would be continued after lunch.

On large open stoves, the ladies had begun steaming the afore-mentioned leaf bhajias, muthias, which are prepared with rice and flour. The indispensable *khichdi* was always on any farm menu, spicy baingan (aubergine) as a veg accompaniment, butter milk (lassi), mango juice undiluted – which is part of the main meal – and the meal would be rounded off with fresh fruit recently picked by the workers.

The juniors have a naughty titter ...

After lunch, the whole party toured the orchards for a favourite pastime: fruit picking.

The generous hosts provided them with *kikapu* (baskets) and the kids needed no encouragement in filling their booty by the sack-full!

All of a sudden, everyone heard a shout and then a scream. A most amazing sight came into view. Dr Shah was running, it seemed, for dear life shouting, 'Help, I've got the ants.' Yes, the doctor had 'ants in his pants,' quite literally! During this season, the area was infested with black ants known as the *siafu*. They usually appear after the rains, endless little armies on the veranda and other interiors as well as the garden and if you were not extra careful you were liable to pick some of the creatures along with the fruit!! Fortunately for him the doctor picked up only a few but there are horrifying tales of these creatures devouring, unfortunate humans and animals in whole!

A couple of the dads, including Shekhar's, along with the host caught up with the poor victim to ascertain how to help, but the man could not stand still, shrieking away and beginning to remove one of his garments after another. Shekhar and Nilesh, using a bit of initiative, rushed to get hold of Juma the foreman and any available farm worker and by the time they reached the scene of 'transgression' everyone witnessed, albeit reluctantly, a full Monty, for the ants had invaded 'private territory,' it seemed.

The ladies hid their faces with embarrassment and moved away but the younger kids had a real naughty giggle, particularly as the victim was who he was. 'Doctor Uncle,' you see, was never flavour of the month with the children as his presence, mostly a home (medical) visit meant *sindhano* (injection) time, since it was only when fever or such illnesses occurred that he appeared to be around.

'Hush, you naughty children,' whispered the mums. 'It's nothing to laugh about, can't you see Uncle is in pain, and besides, he is always around when you are ill, whether you appreciate his method of treatment or not.'

It was the doctor who had now become the patient as a lot of body area was red with the ant stings. Mrs Shah had gone berserk from the onset, when she had to witness her man in his state, probably for the first time, as he was always the cool and collected 'Doctor Saheb'. The apologetic host, though not the least in guilt, along with Juma, and others, applied emergency as well as rural ointments, and after a while all the commotion subsided, particularly with the ladies.

It was nearly tea-time and the guests prepared to leave, pacifying their embarrassed hosts repeatedly as to the late afternoon's events! Mr Engineer mentioned as an aside to the host and the others, 'one really needs to be careful, I remember visiting a friend overnight at his *shamba* some time ago and finding a huge spider in my shoe in the morning!' For the group, it was some time before another farm visit was planned and under-taken.

One thing was certain, though, Doctor Saheb would indulge in every activity at the farm, except fruit pick-ing!!

Chapter 9

K.K.

Among all of the family's friends and acquaintances, the one Shekhar admired most was "uncle" K.K. As seen in previous chapters, whenever the Vakils were on an outing, K.K. Desai (full name Kishorebhai Kashibhai Desai), or K.K. as he was affectionately known, would invariably be invited to accompany them.

The gentleman was a prominent lawyer in Mombasa and his friendship with Shekhar's dad became the stuff of legends and the talk of Indian social circles. Although they were not childhood friends as such, having met late in life, most people would have thought otherwise.

Dad often used to joke or tease his friend about the fascination as well as convenience of initials as an abbreviation for full names, in the Patel/Desai community.

'You chaps are so many in number, and with similar names, rather like the Smiths with the English, the only way to distinguish each other is by identifying the second (father's) initial and even that sometimes doesn't suffice! Shekhar finds it particularly amusing as he says the abbreviations remind him of film gangsters, or shady characters who are often portrayed as such!'(K.K., J.J., J.B. ...)

A further source of mirth was when he first met him and had to address his elder in the traditional way was the slightly tongue twisting "k k *kaka!* (uncle). He thus invariably addressed him as simply uncle *Kishore*.

K.K. however, did not have an ounce of shadiness about him. Years later, Shekhar's recollections of this highly likeable, ethical man remained vivid as he mentioned them to his own off-spring.

Physically, he was not too striking, of average height and build. His most noteworthy facet was his disarming smile. Although quite intense most of the time, when he broke into smile, it was genuine and one felt at once at ease with him.

K.K. the colourful, as Dad sometimes called his friend, loved to paint and loved his garden, and was a connoisseur of the bougainvillea, the rose and the *raat rani* (queen of the night). The man ensured that the gardener, who was selected after thorough scrutiny gave all the 'tender, loving care' that was required for his Eden to become the prized showpiece which it eventually turned into, over a period.

The barrister, donning resplendent white sharkskin/linen suits invariably embellished with a red rose on his lapel-breast was a familiar sight at the courts and often referred to as 'the man with the rose' or, to his often, poor African clients as *'Vakili wa maua'* – lawyer of/with the flower.

The position had not been acquired easily, as he had had to borrow funds to go to the UK to study law. He had limited time but he managed being called to the Bar within the stipulated two years and returned to Kenya. It was obvious to all that he became friends with Dad initially due to their common profession. They never seemed to get tired of each other's company, and people joked about their – almost – 24/7 friendship, as not only were they seen together at weekend outings but daily evenings and ordinary weekends too were spent in each others' company

Shekhar, therefore, once when he was fairly young, asked Dad, who was alone for a change about this. 'Just what is it about uncle Kishore that is so great, which draws you to him? And what do you talk about all the time?'

Dad smiled and told his son at least some of the specialities of the man and incidences. 'Well, Son, we obviously discuss law ... and ... his garden although I'm not a particular enthusiast, but first I'll tell you some interesting tales about him. You might not remember, but a few years ago he went to the U.K. to qualify as a barrister. His benefactor, a wealthy member of his community funded his trip and upon his return, K.K. set up his own practice and one person he employed was the former's son. On one occasion, the young man, taking things for granted, misbehaved with one of the secretaries. The most everyone expected was a reprimand, but my friend, without a moment's hesitation called the young man and handed him his final pay cheque!

'On another occasion, we were driving along the prominent Kilindini Road, in his recently acquired American Limousine when a Colonial, shouted a racist remark at us. "Just mind the car for a moment," he said to me, alighted, walked over, and before the chap had time to recover, landed his right palm across his cheek in front of the stunned members of the public! Walking back totally unruffled, he resumed his position behind the wheel and carried on the journey, "just a little something I had to take care of," he grinned ...'

Hearing such tales, it was no wonder that Shekhar's respect for his father's mate increased two-fold. One of the most amazing characteristics Shekhar found about his object of admiration was that in spite of his almost religious fervour to his fellow man, high principles and feelings for the downtrodden and those less fortunate than himself, the man was a confirmed atheist. As Dad clarified, 'I suppose he doesn't mind the ladies of the household practising religion, but I'm sure he has never entered a temple nor uttered a religious prayer since he attained maturity.' He continued, 'It was quite amusing when a *Swami* (sage), on a visit from the sub-continent, happened quite ironically to be put up at K.K.'s place due to family connections. Being quite unaware of his host's anti-beliefs, the Swami on the first morning, requested materials to light a *'diva'* (spiritual lamp).

The host replied, 'The only lamp you will find in my abode is the electrical one on the ceiling,' as he pointed upwards. Needless to say, the guest requested and was granted, a change of abode that very evening! ...

K.K. lived life to the full and shared his pleasures with others.

Dinners at 'Ajay Nivas,' for that was how the family abode was known, were lavish, grand affairs. The bungalow itself was finely built: large rooms, stylish furniture and of course the immaculate garden. Although a teetotaller (and strict vegetarian) himself, the host saw to it that guests had a ready supply of whisky and cigars.

Geeta said to her brother, 'It's really wonderful to see him looking after his guests, the only drink I have seen him taking is tap water. The huge Kelvinator fridge at their home is packed with stainless steel jars containing cold water and uncle stands with his feet outstretched and guzzles down almost a litre at a go!' she giggled.

'And their living room, my, imported furniture and artefacts to go with it. Uncle seems to have a fascination with things oriental. There are geisha dolls, oriental pottery and the cupboard is packed with those small red pills – the mouth refreshers – *jintan.*'

One evening the family heard a car horn blasting repeatedly. The children rushed outside. One of the kids was sitting on K.K.'s lap and horning away.

Shekhar announced, '*Kishore* uncle has got himself a

new Pontiac, it's a turquoise blue, super leather interiors, and ivory to match.'

'When are you taking us on a safari in your new car?' a couple of the younger siblings asked simultaneously.

'Whenever you wish, we can go to Malindi next week,' replied the elder. Despite his otherwise intense style, he could become child-like when occasion demanded. On birthdays, each of the children got presents befitting their age, but the two elder cousins, had a special present. As soon as they touched their elder's feet, out came a 100-shilling note or the colonial equivalent, an affectionate slap on the back with a subtle wink, 'share it with others.'

'Needless to say uncle, it'll all be spent after friends at our party,' was the boys' standard reply.

One night Dad and K.K. sat very late discussing some legal issue. Everyone wondered what was going on. When Mum asked, of course details were not given but Dad told her the outline. 'You know how we always endeavour to help the less affluent, especially the native who often can't afford legal fees and my friend feels for them more than even I do. I cannot divulge names but a couple of days ago an African came to see my friend since his son has been charged with attempted rape of an Indian girl by a well-known family.'

'Oh God,' sighed Mum, the most sensitive of the elders, and sat down on the sofa.

'The complication is,' continued Dad, both the parties are known to Kishorebhai. He has known the native for years, who used to work in a relative's garage and my friend says he can absolutely vouch for the man's integrity knowing how he has brought up his children and the young man charged also used to run errands for the family during school holidays. What's more he has already interviewed both.

K.K. really had a fight on his hands, since Syed, the accused's father begged him to defend, '*Bwana, saidiya*

tafadhali. Mungu tuta lipa mwenge,' (please help, bwana, God will replenish aplenty).

The expected reply was, 'I do not need any blessings
from your God, but I shall do what I can.'

Members of the community were aghast when they
discovered who the defence lawyer was and the latter
knew he would not make a few enemies, especially as
the opposite party was very prominent and influential
in Mombasa's Asian Community.

Finally, it came down to the repressed and hypocriti-
cal values of those times not only in western but much
more in eastern society, whereby girls were virtually
locked in and social contact with the opposite sex was
monitored by certain sections of the community (the
ultra 'religious' or the ultra 'respected') ruthlessly. On
occasions such as this one therefore it was the least
'expected' who managed to create a furore. In court the
clever lawyer succeeded in proving to the shocked gathering under cross examination that it was the girl who
visited the young man at anomalous hours. When the
worst was suspected, she cried 'rape.'

A short time later, Dad advised, 'The family have sent
the girl away, but I suspect for a long time to come it
will only be our family and a select few who will associ-
ate with this man of principles,' referring to his friend
who had never feared anything or anyone come what
may.

The good die young is an oft occurred truism and in the
case of this great and gutsy man that is what happened.

A few years later, the Vakil family had shifted to
Nairobi, the two friends always remaining in touch via
phone and occasional visits. They had a special way of
greeting each other on the phone – imitating some
religious hypocrite that they both had had a brush with,
but when Dad picked up the phone this particular
morning and there was no such exchange everyone

knew something was amiss.

His dear friend was no more.

K.K. had not completed his 50th but the easy-going life style and weight problems in later years had taken their toll. For the first time Shekhar saw Dad break down and weep openly.

'There was not a thing about myself and my personal life that I did not discuss with him, not one damn thing,' he said to his son, who tried helplessly to comfort his father whilst weeping internally himself ...

Oh yes, their friendship was certainly of the stuff that legends are made, something to write home about. Even after they lived in different parts of the country, Dad thought nothing of sacrificing his relations with members of his own community whose pettiness came in the way of their friendship.

The fragrance of the man has remained over the years and indeed remains to date, not unlike that of his prize garden which he so lovingly tended whilst he was around ...

Chapter 10

New Decade. New home.

The 1950s had arrived. Decade of hope, optimism, new ideas and aspirations. The war years were firmly behind for the world at large, although new and smaller wars unfortunately kept cropping up as in the Korean War and the beginning of the Cold War. In Kenya, a state of emergency was declared in 1952 with the Mau-Mau struggle for independence, violent and brutal at times. With India's independence in 1947, other colonies were obviously inspired to follow suit, by whichever means, and here, Jomo Kenyatta, the London educated Kikuyu Leader became the guiding force.

At the coast, however, there was comparatively little tension and certainly none for the younger set. Shekhar and family moved into the new house and our lad started primary school. These were the years of simple and lesser learning and more play. (The age of comic books, the *Beano* and *Dandy* weeklies, with Dennis the Menace and Roger the Dodger!), the pocket-sized black and white westerns (Davy Crockett and Kit Carson), and of course Marvel's Superman and Batman. Finally, there was Indian material too, *Chandamama* (and the more contemporary *Ramakdoo*) with stories and pictures of historical and fictitious noble characters, entertainment with enlightenment for the young.

In the evenings, it was playing with marbles, *gili danda*, the Indian stick and mini skittle game and of course tennis-ball cricket, although Shekhar and his age group were still novices at all this. Then there was 'The Saturday morning picture show' with the B picture westerns of stars such as war veteran Audie Murphy and Randolph Scott. On the 'Eastern front' you had the swashbucklers of Ranjan, he of the curly locks and of course, pencilled moustache!

When the Vakils finally acquired their own law practice they decided to move out of town and into the suburban area of Tudor, a more exclusive part of the Mombasa island city. The new house had five bedrooms, two bathrooms, a beautiful open sun terrace, leading onto a rear sunken garden, which continued to the left side rear and then led to a pebble and sand area with medium sized trees bearing the scented and white 'champa' and 'karrain' flowers, the latter in yellow/white as well as pink/white. There were a few flower beds hosting hibiscus and other plants common to the coast. The rear garden was rectangular and wide, mostly lawned and at the end came the four-foot wall which ran across all the houses. This was obviously for child safety as well as possible (small) animal prevention from the bush area which covered the space all the way down to the sea. The beach here was tolerable but not ideal for swimming.

Access to the beach was by way of a long walk through grassland and various kinds of shrubbery and a small selection of jack fruit trees. You finally reached the top of the narrow strip of a dusty path, which you either slid or walked down and finally reached the bottom. What you came upon was well worth the long trek that you would have just undertaken. The view, although not exactly a bather's paradise, displayed a large expanse of water, Nyali Bridge in the distance and the far end with lots of greenery, not to speak of palm trees plus walkers with dogs, occasional sea gulls flying about and the odd adventurous bathers all of which did not disappoint.

On the right of the bungalow as you entered were the servant's quarters where Ali and Osman stayed. Adjoining was a car port. The front was a large square area with a lawn section plus some medium sized yellow variety of palm trees, thriving naturally in the sand terrain, which gave a natural, coastal feel to the overall landscape, including the rest of the gardens. Osman, since the fiasco with the Car had wised up considerably and besides his known skills he proved to be a competent gardener, which was just as well, since all the four adults in the house, including the busy menfolk were garden lovers.

Dineshchandra (Shekhar's dad) somehow never mastered the Swahili language whereas *Kakaji* spoke it almost like a native, and listening to Dad speaking broken Kiswahili – and that is an understatement – along with nearly 90 percent English was a cause of mirth to anyone present:

Father: *Wewe* (you) dig that plot and put some more *maua* (flower plants/flower) roses as it looks empty.

Osman: Yes *bwana*.

F: and *alafu wewe ..., wewe*, do the same for that *angini* patch *huko*.

O: Yes, *bwana mkuba*.

F: *alafu*, – and now running out of vocabulary and upon being rescued by mother's arrival on the scene – Shanta can you please tell Osman to trim that overgrown hedge?

O: (in anticipation) *ndio, mama ...*

The delight of the ladies and ultimately the menfolk too – when they had the time and were allowed in this ladies' restricted zone, was the substantial vegetable patch, concealed all round with a hedge. *Kakiji*, in her respectful but authoritative school ma'am tones was often heard chiding her surreptitiously investigative husband, who upon apprehension, '*Arre kya baat hai,*

Bhanu, you ladies have created a farmer's paradise here, we never realised ... aubergines, *karelas,* (bitter gourd) various bean, sweet potato ... pocket and palate both are going to benefit.' To which *Kakiji* would reply, 'Well, as long as the examination is very short, if you please, those vines (of the cucumber plant) are **most** delicate!'

The bungalow itself was located as a large corner plot and was within what one might call a huge estate of residences. There were narrow, un-tarmacked roads with grass shoots between the tyre markings and lots of open spaces around the housing with palm and cashew nut trees as well as the jack fruit tree. Finally, on the far right there was the Nyali Bridge linking the island with the North coast, affluent Nyali area and beyond.*

Esmail the driver continued to provide his services, which were now indispensable, as the house was a fair distance from township and schools.

---

* The Nyali city which was planned during the 70s is now in existence and being self-sufficient one can arrive and depart by air without, if so required, going into Mombasa town/island.

Chapter 11

Growing up with Ali – the later years ...

When the family had moved to the suburban house, Ali saw the perfect opportunity to shape up his protégé as well as the cousin, physically, considering their puny frames which he had often commented upon.

'*Mambo una taka ku badirishwa, vijana, nyinyi ni mwanaume ... ao wanawake?*' (things need to change, young men, are you men ... or women?)

At last one Saturday, the nine year olds were woken up suddenly from their morning slumber, '*Kumar, Nilesh, amuka u/pesi,*' (get up quickly) whispered Ali so as not to wake the others.

'Oh, come on *Mwalimu*, it's Saturday,' protested the boys but they were ignored. Compelled to dress quickly, still rubbing their eyes, moaning and cursing softly they were jogged to the beach and after a few mild workouts returned. Raw egg in milk, followed by hot porridge was going to be the daily breakfast. 'So remember, every day it's up with the lark and off we'll go, just as we did today.' Osman – Ali's nephew – who had started at the second house also joined them occasionally. After the first few days of cursing and whining the boys began to enjoy their sessions which were gradually intensified as time went by.

When Shekhar was in his late teens, stout and almost a six-footer, he often reflected fondly upon these sessions, which had started the boys off on their love for physical workouts and sport.

Playing with matches

One afternoon, during the height of the dry season, the cousins became restless and decided to get up to a bit of mischief. They got hold of a box of matches and climbed over the four-foot wall separating the garden from the grassland and shrubs leading downwards to the beach and began their task. The grass section was dry and they began setting it alight, putting out the fire just as it appeared to get out of hand. Each time the flames got bigger, and finally at one stage it became uncontrollable.

The fire spread fast and soon it had reached the neighbours' side as well. The boys panicked, shouting to Mum and the workers, 'Ali, Osman there's a fire.' Shekhar's mum had been taking a siesta in the guest room by the garden and at first thought it was rain, but then thought better, 'Not in this season,' she said to herself.

Ali and others from the neighbourhood brought sand, large buckets and used garden hoses to put out the flames.

Luckily, the grassland width was not so huge which then adjoined the comparatively green shrubbery and trees as well.

In the midst of all the commotion the boys had to pull a 'fast one' and quickly too. 'Mum, Ali, we only saw the fire after it had already started, probably one of the young boys staying nearby ...' Somehow neither the parents, when the remaining members had arrived in the evening, nor Ali and co believed the story.

Thrashing the truth out from children was not part of the family trait so the slow method was adopted. For the next several days, at every available opportunity each of the parents brought up the subject, veering the conversation and asking the boys knowingly, 'Shekhar, Nilesh, what do you reckon would be a fitting punishment for the culprits, were we to get hold of them?'

The response was always the same; innocent faces, hunched shoulders and looking at each other. Finally, it was left to Ali to get the facts. He called the boys to the quarters one evening and after a long talk eyeing them closely said, 'We all know who started the fire, don't we, *Vijana?* How long do you boys want to go on living this lie? You must go and tell the parents, however bitter the outcome may be. Believe me the punishment won't be half as bad as you think.'

The boys owned up that very evening and apologised. 'Sorry, daddy, *Kakaji*, we were responsible for the fire and we also apologize for the lie and not owning up earlier.' Sure enough they were punished, just as Ali had said.

And sure enough, the punishment, which amounted to no Saturday morning pictures with the mates and no playtime for a few weeks somehow seemed not half as cruel or bad as they had feared, just as their mentor had promised.

Ali thus had a big embrace waiting for him next morning from the boys before their beach session ...

Shades of the admirable Crichton (the perfect butler)
... or ... Jeeves, perhaps ...?

Having worked for a number of years at the Englishman's home, as he had informed the family earlier, Ali had acquired quite a few useful talents. One evening Shekhar's dad and *Kakaji* announced to the rest of the family: 'We're holding a cocktail party this Saturday, inviting a few friends as well as clients. The law practice is going very well and a number of new clients have been acquired; inform the workers. Ali is always going on about his skills at the bar and non-veg items, let's see.'

So that evening, Ali became the perfect Butler, dressed in simple white and the standard scarlet Arabic cap he took charge of the bar mixing drinks with ease and expertise and also managed to prepare non-vegetarian items, in addition to the barbeque which young Osman also handled with ease and expertise.

The party was a grand success, held in the rear garden with the sea view and Nyali Bridge as backdrop.

'How on earth did you manage to get hold of this fellow, Vakil?' Dad was asked repeatedly by the guests, who were obviously highly impressed with Ali's conduct most becoming, throughout the evening.

'Yes, Ali is a great asset to the household. Between him and his nephew Osman, they practically run the entire domestic show, indispensable to each house member in a unique way,' said *Uncleji*, while the womenfolk were occupied elsewhere, of course!

Later that evening, having observed their expertise at the bar, the 'butlers' were rewarded with a couple of bottles of Scotch and a wink, by the *bwanas*.

Chapter 12

School days ...

Along with Ali's 'special education', the older boys Shekhar and Nilesh were enrolled in primary school whilst the family still lived at 'old town'.

Shekhar was enrolled in the Kitauni primary school (where the elder cousin Nilesh had enrolled the previous year) twinned with Kimauni school. Surprisingly, they had African names. Separated by a long wall with a shared assembly area most of the classes were at ground level – the final year on the upper level. The last year (Year 7) would see the students sit their K.A.P.E. (Kenya Asian Preliminary Exam), the 'A' later dropped for obvious reasons. Shekhar settled down well in his new environment. English was the medium and besides the 3Rs the other main subjects included science (or Nature Study as it was called), Art and ethnic Gujarati as a second language.

The evening before the first day, the family had a small meeting. 'School days, they are the best days of your lives, make the most of them,' was told by the ones who had already been, 'for they will not be offered, like most opportunities, twice. Yes, young man, amidst the occasional tear or two, the odd bullying, if you are unlucky enough and nastiness even by some teacher, there will be lots of learning, play and young camaraderie with new found friends. Good times, times to savour,' The elders finished their short lecture and the new students retired for the night, wondering what would be in store next day.

Friendships that evolve during childhood often last a lifetime. During these primary school years Shekhar met Dilip, Arif, Indrajeet (Singh), friendships which withstood the test of time. Even today, in some North London club, the four would be meeting on a Friday evening to reminiscence about old times, over a pint or two. There was always the class comedian and for most of the years Shekhar had Mukund the *mote* or *jadiyo* (fatty) for entertainment. Mukund loved his food, of course, and had a jovial nature.

During breaks his mates often teased, 'So what's for second breakfast today, Mukund, samosa, potato bhajia or are you taking a "break"?' 'Not half a chance,' would be the reply, to the last option and off he would go to the head of the canteen queue for his quota of the goodies, usually two in each hand along with Coke to wash them down. Being primary, the school was co-ed, but at this stage in life, the sexes usually grouped to their own socially, except in study matters.

Shekhar always made it a point to go early and had a pact with Esmail to drive him to town, first. After his early, healthy breakfast - courtesy Ali, he had to top it up with something tasty.

His mates in town would be waiting and once Shekhar arrived, they went straight to the 'Bhadala' Bhajia woman. She had a small place in an alley and the first round of piping hot (in more ways than one!) bhajias was reserved for her young customers. *'Haraka, vijana, chunga joto'* (hurry, boys, careful, they're hot). First time that Esmail was asked to drive to the outlet, Shekhar pleaded with his smiling chauffeur, 'Please don't tell Ali, you know he is very strict about my diet, since we have started the exercise routine, I promise we won't come here *every* day,' he pledged.

At school, the assemblies were conducted under the Union Jack with *God save the Queen* and it would be a further decade plus, before independent Kenya's schools began singing *E'Mungu nguvu zetu* (O God of all creation, bless this our land and nation ...). The teachers at school were a varied and interesting cross-section and by the time the 'gang of four' had reached the senior primary years, most of their 'imparters of knowledge' had, with some special exceptions, given a good account of themselves.

Mr Rebeiro taught English Language. He was strict but fair and once you were in his good books he did his best to encourage you. Tall and athletic looking, he had a smart upright gait and an overall manner which demanded deference from his students. Except for his archetypal Goan pronunciations, his English was impeccable in all respects. During the last couple of years, Shekhar tuned to Mr Rebeiro very well and the English class became a favourite.

In the early years, Art under Miss Shah and Gujarati under Mr P.P. Patel were generally popular with students. Our lad had a natural talent, it seemed, for drawings and when one fine morning he declared his artistic intentions by mentioning to his adults at home that he would want to be a professional painter, everyone took it in with a bit of mirth. 'Look *Bhabhiji*,' said Father, 'your nephew has clearly inherited his ancestors' artistic talents like yourself, but as for taking it to a new level, we'll have to wait and see,' he laughed. Miss Shah, otherwise gentle and patient could very occasionally have a burst out with students who took art as a cartoon session (some of whom nicknamed her Mickey Mouse – meaning Minnie Mouse). She was like an elder sister that Shekhar never had and her encouragement was greatly appreciated.

As for the Gujarati class – this was in the days before you had to take French, Latin or Swahili as a second language – it was under the flagship of *Kaka* (Uncle), as

P.P. was nicknamed. A good-natured fellow, of medium height with crop cut hair, and large horn-rimmed spectacles which gave him the look of a German commandant except that in nature, he was anything but. His loose trousers almost always kept falling off, as he often forgot or lost his waist-belt and thus used one of his old ties as substitute, invariably hid behind the jacket. Of course, this did not prevent him from constantly pushing up his trousers, during lesson, with his palm edges!!

During class, whilst speaking or dictating, he would look out the window, presumably in the direction of his home town in the sub-continent, with a lost expression, all the while caressing the top of one of his palms with the other hand's index finger in a circular motion.

It was a real *piece-de-resistance*, the day when the class joker, in P.P.'s short absence, encouraged by his co-students did a *Kaka* impression, his favourite, complete with a string piece to substitute for the tie.

'Come on Mukund, let's see your "class" act,' enthused the girls.

'We challenge you,' said the boys.

The comic in him motivated enough, up went Mukund on the table. The delighted giggles of the girls and derisive hoots of the boys came to an abrupt end, however, as P.P. returned quite suddenly. In a rare and angry outburst, he lifted 'Motey' off the table and by the scruff, hissing, 'Come on Johnny Walker' (the master film comic during those days), 'Teacher's going to teach you some **real** comedy now,' this action almost throwing both of them onto the floor — resulting in further but suppressed laughter from the class!

Then there was Mr Hussein the arithmetic teacher, a gentler person you would never find and a total contrast to some others. His favourite words of encouragement to any pupil with a difficulty would be '*koi baat nahin, aa jayega*' (no problem, we'll find a solution). He took real pains to teach the weaker students and the pass rate for all his classes was nearly 100 per cent.

All students must have observed at some time or the other that there is invariably one or two among the profession, who seem to almost enjoy imparting punishment along with knowledge. Times have changed as have teaching methods, though not in all parts of the world but, in those days, it was often a case of 'double punishment' if you dared to protest, (for the boys anyway). A parent often gave you a dose of the same *medicine* if, upon reaching home you complained about a teacher's thrashing in class/school!!

Mr Pawar, then, was the Assistant Head Teacher and a scourge of the pupil. In appearance, he was fair, blue-eyed, heavy and of medium height; except for his weight one would have probably called him handsome. He used to enter class huffing and puffing, banging his books onto the table and invariably after a few seconds of quizzical looks, would inquire, in his rounded Punjabi accent: '*How* are we all? Have we progressed since we last met?' to which a unanimous reply would come in a 30-odd chorus, loud, but docile and clear, 'Yes, Sir.'

Mr Pawar taught geography, not everybody's favourite and even less so due to this teacher. He gave lots of home-work and woe betide any student who dared not submit it in time. By the final year things came to a head and became quite unbearable as he was quite intimidating to the girls as well as the boys whenever opportunity arose. Yes, it did seem as if this sadist enjoyed punishing his pupils. Then quite by chance, Shekhar and his mates discovered through one of the girls, whose mother was a junior class teacher that all was not well on the home-front for the assistant head and that he was rather 'close' to Miss Bhatia, the junior history teacher. By now, the students were old enough to understand this to a large extent and waited for their chance. Due to his varied duties as teacher/assistant head/head substitute when required for the aged school Principal and domestic problems, he often ran late for his timetable and thus passed secret messages to the lady in question, through a junior pupil. When this was finally discovered by the gang, a couple of the lads managed to intercept the note one day and jointly confronted Mr Pawar.

'Sir, we have found this note, you see and we can't quite pinpoint the writing although they do seem familiar so we thought, um ... we would, um ... just hand it to the Head and let him deal with it,' mumbled Shekhar and Indrajit, in rather sheepish tones. The blackmailed party, at first wanting to threaten, but then thinking the better of it, shocked beyond belief, with blood draining from his face, by the minute, made one last stand, 'I don't suppose you boys would consider handing the note to me?' Came the clever reply, 'Well, Sir, we wouldn't want to be accessories to anything the Head would disapprove of.' Realising he was beaten, the Assistant Head finally accepted all the usual terms, in such, albeit rare, circumstances. No more intimidation, fair treatment and early departures home in cases of urgency, whether real or otherwise, were all agreed to. Needless to say, the note was hidden away safely, just in case.

Today one often talks of family values or the lack of them in present day society. However, the so called 'family values' and moral standards were not always so high as one now hears about or reads in the media with hindsight, even in those seemingly innocent days. Due to media censorship as well as, to an extent, double standards and social hypocrisy, things often got brushed under the carpet.

'Weirdos' existed even in those days, of course, and Kitauni had a narrow escape with one of these. Mr Jani, the new teacher seemed very nice in all respects. Middle-aged and immaculately dressed, often in double-breasted cream coloured shark skin suits, which were apparently very popular in the tropics at the time, always smiling and very soft spoken. First time they saw him, one of his friends asked Shekhar, 'Did you see that new history master? The fancy dude with the perennial smile. Jani, I think his name is.'

'Johnny more likely,' laughed Shekhar, 'He teaches history to the final year and I hear he's not a bad teacher, either.'

One day however, Dilip accidentally happened to see him at finishing time of one of the final classes with a female pupil. Under the pretext of tutoring, obviously confident of no one else's presence, he appeared to be in a compromising pose, his hands around, and what was quite apparent, his embarrassed pupil. 'The rascal was almost embracing the poor girl, and there wasn't a thing she could do about it,' said a clearly shocked and furious Dilip. From then onwards, the mates were vigilant.

It was the Annual Sports Day. By now, in the penultimate year Shekhar had developed an interest in and a fair amount of proficiency at, a number of activities including high jump and athletics. Sports houses in schools had African themes. In some schools you had them named after explorers of Africa, such as Livingstone, Stanley or Burton. Here at Kitauni the theme was wildlife: *Simba, Chui, Kifaru, Ndovu.* (Lion, Cheetah, Rhinoceros, Elephant). Dilip and Shekhar had managed to win the odd prize and after the event made their way to the gates. Suddenly Shekhar saw Mr Jani with the female pupil walking to the parking lot for the teachers' cars. Earlier, he had seen the former around the events to his surprise as sports and this teacher had nothing in common. Promising his friend with a quick 'See you later, I've just spotted old Johnny round the corner, I'm sure something's amiss,' the young hero followed the suspect to the cars. By now the school was almost deserted; all except Mr Ribeiro who was also the sports master and a couple of co-ordinators who had remained to round off.

After the earlier event Shobha (the pupil) had been warned by the friends to keep her distance and it was puzzling now to see her alone with the Master at this hour. They sat in the teacher's two-door Morris, for what seemed an eternity as an exasperated Shekhar watched and waited from behind a wall. The teacher's charms and tactics had worked thus far, however it seemed the girl was at last resisting what appeared to be his suggestion of them driving away together. There appeared to be some sort of a tussle and the young man did not wait further. He sprinted towards the sports pavilion and spotting Mr Rebeiro requested him amid gasps to come with him immediately.

'What's the matter, boy?' the latter queried, but there was no time or words, for that matter, to explain, 'Sir, please, Sir, Mr Jani, Shobha. I can't explain.' There was urgency as well as embarrassment in the pupil's voice. They rushed to the parking lot.

In a moment the situation was sized up, since in the locked car a physical struggle, uneven though it was, had ensued. The girl was screaming for help, but her aggressor confident of their sole presence in the parking lot, appeared to be taking liberties with the former's clothing garments. Arriving in the nick of time, with fury and blood shot eyes, the Sports Master banged on the doors; banged and then shook so hard that for a few moments the two-seater rocked from side to side. The culprit, by now aghast, opened the doors, with Shekhar immediately taking the tearful, shaking girl to safety and Mr Rebeiro taking his adversary by the scruff and landing the one and only punch that was necessary to throw him on the ground ... By now the coordinators had arrived and one of them arranged transport home for the two pupils.

All was hush hush at the Assembly next morning. Obviously, nothing was discussed in the open, however the teachers and most final year pupils were aware of the situation. The teacher was grilled for hours, the girl's parents came and questions were asked: 'Did not the school make any checks on backgrounds? This sort of thing had been unheard of, especially with this school's reputation and the Head Teacher's standing itself was on the line. Things cooled down gradually as Mr Jani was made to pack his bags straightaway and face charges, the outcome of which nobody followed or was interested in, although it came as no surprise to the (senior) pupils when one of them overheard from elders that the teacher, years earlier had had a similar problem whilst at a High School.

School bullying, like other forms of harrying, it seems, has existed from the time schools have been around and Kitauni had its share of the species. Sometimes at a class level and occasionally the school bully at large, usually in the final year, who pretended to practically own the school and its (pupil) inhabitants, in so far as the satisfaction of his wishes or fancies were concerned.

Karim Virjee was the classic school bully. Of medium height and leaning on the heavier build, he had an occasionally poker-faced, but mostly an arrogant air about him. You could somehow tell just by a quick glance that here was a spoilt, rich kid who had been allowed to do pretty much what he had fancied. Two years older than Shekhar's group, he was repeating the 7th form – so in effect he was only one year ahead. The poor school – souls had the 'pleasure' of enduring him therefore, for a further year. His family was very prominent in town, big businessmen his father and maternal uncle were. One of his close relatives was also on the school board of Governors, hence the blind eye many teachers turned to the fellow's exploits.

Each morning the 'Boss' as his young cronies called him, arrived in Dad's Chevrolet Limousine, invariably chauffeur driven. He came fairly early, to confer with his 'associates' and plan for the day. One day it was harassing the girls, the next would be reserved for obtaining pupils' pocket money in return for 'protection'. This would be spent on canteen goodies or cigarettes, smoked discreetly behind the sports ground shed.

Shekhar, astutely avoided any encounter with Karim as far as was possible. However, one morning, the former happened to be browsing through the latest issue of a boys' comic. The bully, passing by, just snatched the magazine and continued walking; an argument ensued. 'Give that back to me please,' Shekhar was as polite as possible.

'Make me,' challenged the other. The victim complained to Mr Ribeiro who was by now quite fond of this student; it was nearly the end of the sixth year for him and he was showing signs of serious preparation for the K.A.P.E. due the following year.

The teacher who was normally placid as far as such issues went and avoided them, was easily annoyed if he witnessed injustice. When proof of ownership was provided by the younger student's scribbled remarks on a particular page; no further evidence was required. With his left, the master snatched the book from the culprit and simultaneously whacked an inverted right which sent the boy reeling. '*Yo'all* should be doing something more productive at this stage than fighting over comic books,' he exclaimed and walked away. Karim gave a look before he disappeared off the corridor which read, 'I'm going to get you for this.'

In the event, it was the younger party that was constrained to make the move. Just before the year ended the gang heard how on more than one occasion younger pupils got harassed by the Karim gang. One of the boys, a sensitive lad, often came to the mates for guidance or lifts home.

'All I was doing was having my lunch break with my mates,' complained the boy between his tears 'and, and that ... that ... Karim just snatched my box ... and returned it empty,' he broke down again.

Shekhar could not bear this any longer and it was time for an open confrontation. Despite the difference in stature, a fight was arranged one Friday afternoon after school at the rear of the sports ground behind a shed. Dilip and the others attempted to dissuade their pal, 'Do you realise what you are getting yourself into,' said the Sikh, Indra, who normally took up such challenges. 'Even I, as you know, steer clear of that Goon.' The challenger, however, was adamant.

The fight lasted only a few minutes. Torn shirt, black eye and bleeding nose is what the young hero got. After a patch-up job at one of the friends,' he was dropped off late evening. The womenfolk, particularly *Kakiji* were horror-struck of course; luckily their spouses had still not arrived home. Trusty old Ali intervened, '*Pole, Mama, mimi nita chunga mambo*' (Easy, Madam, I'll take care of the matter). They talked for a while in Ali's quarters. Finally, with a wink the latter said, '*Kesho Subui, kua tayari!*' (Be ready tomorrow morning).

Tarzan to the rescue ...

Next day onwards in addition to their morning beach sessions, Ali gave his young charge a beginner's course in the art of self-defence; a bit of boxing among other things. Not that his wise mentor wanted the student involved in another fight; he just didn't want his protégé to be in a similar situation again. '*Hapaana, joo zaidi, chini kidogo sasa! piga!'* (no, higher, little lower, now! strike ...), went the trainer on and on continuing, 'you see this flat nose and these scars, they weren't acquired boxing with shadows, you need more speed, young man.' Ali was a hard taskmaster. At last, when the pupil seemed ready enough, came the three words Shekhar welcomed, with much relief, 'Training *ova*, (over) Tarzan!'

Shekhar went to sleep that night with mixed feelings, confident after his sessions and yet not totally without feelings of apprehension. As for the man in the loin cloth, he was the icon of the times for every school boy, especially in East Africa and the latest film version had been released only last month, which Shekhar had seen with his mates. When they had come out of the auditorium of Regal cinema, Arif exclaimed, 'Wow, what muscles! What looks and those golden locks, they certainly made the girls swoon!'

'I read in a film mag the other day,' expanded Dilip, who was a keen film buff, that the actor who plays Tarzan used to be a football champion, and in addition to tanning himself regularly, swims and gyms every single day just to keep in tune with the image as well as his predecessor who was an Olympic champion swimmer.

'I'm sure some location shooting must have taken place out here in Kenya, and yet the credits only mentioned U.S.A.?' asked Shekhar.

'Well,' replied Dilip, 'apparently, they did shoot *Tarzan's peril* a few years ago around Mount Kenya and in colour too. However, for some technical reason they lost more than half the colour film, so it's still monochrome for a while.'

Indrajit was grinning, 'Technical problems or no, we all love our Ape Man's adventures; all I can hear in the streets and the playgrounds are the kids beating their chests and performing his yodel cry,' and he proceeded to do a mock.

After what seemed a suitable interval, Shekhar confided to his friends about his thoughts concerning a proposal for a re-match. They were of course horror-struck at the suggestion and obviously considered the worst outcomes. 'Are you gone mad?' said Indrajit. 'Not yet,' chuckled the contender, 'but I have to finish this one way or the other. Well, Tarzan, here we go!' So, finally he tapped his adversary on the shoulder one afternoon and expressed his intentions. The latter was gobsmacked, of course. Guffawing to his pal standing beside him he said, 'Some people just cannot have enough – this idiot wants a rematch! Well, a re-match he shall have,' he finished, looking derogatively at his challenger.

So it was, that the following Friday afternoon, after the school was nearly deserted, amidst the same futile protests, the young hero marched towards the playground with his pals, as did his foe and *his* well-wishers, quite sure in their minds of the outcome, and once again they posted a sentry for look-out and once again under a blazing African sun they started their 'encore'; with one big difference this time. Shekhar was not on the defensive, and despite his comparatively lesser stature he landed effective punches and gifted a bloody nose to his opponent. Shocked and astounded the latter retaliated and the match went on and on with both sides bruised and battered. After cheers and boos of surprise from both camps it was time to call it a day and finally, after the non-participants began throwing themselves in between the two fighters each time they confronted – a popular trick to end such fights – the contest ended.

Karim was dragged away, still kicking and screaming, 'I'll get you yet,' by his cronies. Shekhar was warmly – and with relief – felicitated by his friends. 'What was all that?' asked Dilip clearly bowled over and hardly able to conceal his admiration. 'Well let's just say I did a bit of homework this time,' replied the proud and pleased challenger – between his bruises.

Shekhar just about managed to pacify his elders – with Ali's help – and before he tucked in early he went to his mentor's quarters. The eyes of the protégé were not exactly dry as he mock-punched him good night. Whenever he happened to be in a fix, which wasn't too often thankfully, the trusted Ali would always be around.

'No more fights for a while, OK?' chided his guru, with his raised index.

The episode had a happy ending; for Karim, although not totally reformed as a bully – old habits dying hard and that sort of thing – certainly thought twice before approaching his potential victims henceforth.

The final and seventh year was a little more serious as the K.A.P.E.s approached; however, with a little interest on their part and help all round, the 'gang' did pretty well.

High School, however, would be a slightly different jungle …

Chapter 13

Man's best friend

Having sat for the K.A.P. exams, time was on Shekhar's hands as results would not be announced for a while. Mates Dilip, Arif and a few others were always available for company but going into Mombasa town day in, day out and endless games of cricket began to bore the youngsters.

'What you need Shekhu, is a Doggie companion,' suggested Arif whose family had acquired a dog the previous year.

Like most children, the kids in the family had wanted a pet as they started growing up. Initially the family had gone for kittens, but after the second attempt, whereby one of the family elders had to sit up all night with a meowing creature, a decision was taken: 'No more pets!'

The children had let things cool off for a few months. However, when there was a burglary reported in the neighbourhood Shekhar and Nilesh managed to convince the male elders to get a puppy, citing Arif's family as an example. Of course, no attempts were spared at dissuasion, to no avail. Among other things: 'You know the work involved, exercising, bathing, food,' and to the younger ones, 'Did you know that the average life span of a dog is only twelve years! Burglars often poison the dogs,' and so on ... After considering various breeds the family went for a mix-breed that appeared 75 percent Alsatian or German Shepherd, known for its qualities as a guard dog, often used by the police.

As Prafulbhai (*kakaji*) joked, 'We cannot very well go for any of the vicious looking breeds, effective though they may be, as guards, chances are they will probably frighten our lady folk or guests more than any prospective intruders!' When the new member of the family arrived, Father, who had done some research advised, 'Due to the breed's trait of being a one-person dog it is decided that Ali will be responsible for him, until further notice.' For a long period, the latter became a master and friend to the arrival known simply as '*umbwa* or dog'.

The children all doted over him, the girls carrying him around whenever they had the chance and the boys allowing him to sleep in their beds until the mums chased them. Ali made sure the puppy was kept clean, exercised and fed properly. The family took him to their Sunday seaside outings. The first time the boys threw a ball into the sea and waited for a retrieve, the younger girl siblings shouted, 'No, Shekhar, *bhai*, he will drown, please catch him!' The boys, had a good laugh, pretending to panic and then explained, 'Easy, Radha, Reshma, dogs are born natural swimmers,' and sure enough the puppy was back with his prize in no time.

One day, a few months later, and the puppy was growing up fast, as lunch was being prepared consisting of meat and *ugali* Shekhar was shocked to discover what seemed like a bee or wasp mixed into the food. 'Relax, *Kijana*,' said the veteran, 'I have intentionally mixed *nyuki* (bee) in. It makes him *umbwa, kali sana!* (very fierce dog) and brave as a Lion or *Simba*.' Thus 'dog' henceforth came to be known by all as Simba. Gradually, Simba also began transferring his attentions and affection to young Shekhar with walks facing the Nyali Beach and throwing himself with abandon into the water fetching ball or stick being a favourite pastime.

On one occasion Shekhar noticed Simba chewing his favourite toy food, a bone, whereupon he asked Ali, 'what's so tasty about bones that dogs like so much?'

His guru replied, 'It will surprise you, but the sharp bone hits against the dog's gums making them bleed. The dog thinks the blood is oozing from the bone and continues with his snack at leisure!'

The forest and vegetation area, leading down to the sea, as well as the beach itself had no shortage of bird life and Ali, with Osman and the elder cousins often made bird shooting expeditions, which were of course not particularly approved by the elders. The first time after moving into this house, Ali and Osman, returning from their home town, Malindi, brought supplies of special wood. 'Sasa tuta tengeneza Mshali,' (now we shall make bow and arrow) said the elder, to the two excited young onlookers. 'First the bow out of the soft and flexible wood and then the arrows out of the hard one. Then we insert feathers at the rear, with the three cuts, and finally after sharpening the front tips, with the spare bowstring, we create a pattern on the front third of the arrow.' So saying, he lit a small fire and having tied the string on the arrow in a criss-cross shape, made a pattern, by mildly heating the wood. When the string was removed and discarded, it left a brown pattern on the burned part. The delight and admiration was clearly apparent on the boys' faces.

One weekend afternoon, they shot a substantial number of birds, with Simba enjoying himself enormously, retrieving the target both in the tree area as well as the beach. Although some of the shoot was used for culinary purposes by the house workers, Kakaji got wind of the expedition and called the boys. A long lecture followed on wildlife protection, conservation and indeed the Hindu philosophy of nonviolence in any form. 'How could you boys have taken part in such an expedition. Think of the mothers of the baby birds you may have killed and vice-versa.' Shame-faced, the boys went to sleep and after a long thought and discussion resolved not to repeat such an incident. Henceforth the bow and arrows were strictly used for target practice.

One evening, the relative calm of the neighbourhood turned really noisy with a dog fight. A neighbour's Labrador normally quite a friendly breed – to humans at least – and Simba, found themselves unchained. Both being males, the initial growling turned into a full two-way attack. As both families shouted to their canines in vain, for a good part of ten minutes, Ali came to the rescue, suggesting the neighbour to do the same, he shouted to the elder brothers: 'Grab Simba's hind legs and drag like mad, moving all the time, otherwise ...!!'

As the fight was at last broken up, everybody sighed with relief. 'God almighty,' exclaimed Nilesh, 'Had we not kept moving fast, I felt Simba was going to snap my hand off, forgetting who was master!' They nursed the wounds; torn ear, bleeding gums and miniature gashes all over, it was quite a task, what with the twin toddlers of the family who had been incessantly wailing away throughout the sordid episode, seeing their pet pooch in such a state!

Subsequent to a mini-meeting between the elders and the two workers a strong fence was built around the compound. Walking routines were changed to avoid a possible re-occurrence of such a situation. For the most part it worked well; except for the chicken incident, that is.

One of the younger siblings, along with young Osman, was visiting friends nearby. A much-embarrassed Osman related the story later to the elders. 'I was momentarily chatting to one of the lady workers when suddenly Simba decided to tear himself loose and amuse himself by getting acquainted to the chicken brood in the servants' quarters. I did not know whether to laugh or cry, and it was a case of dog chasing brood, boy chasing dog, the *Aya* (house maid) chasing boy plus dog, and in a rage with stick; round and round the compound they went until I managed to get hold of our *umbwa* – just – but not before scraping my arms and knees in the process.' He showed these, as if to gain some sympathy. 'Luckily there was fencing all round, or else the egg-layers would have been chased all the way to Nyali, who knows?'

The two mums, possibly because of their conservative background earlier at the sub-continent had never taken to the pet, whereas everybody else adored him. It took a near-tragedy to change all that. The twins were hardly three at the time and *Kakiji*, who true to her austerity had never made it a secret that she wasn't exactly a fan was busy in the kitchen. The older children were busy playing *santa-kukdi* (hide-and-seek), when one toddler strayed outside the compound. The small dusty road outside luckily did not invite speedy vehicles however, the car would have taken the child, had it not been for the canine's protective sixth sense. The child was pushed away, but a yelp made the household aware of the calamity. In his heroism, the dog had managed to get his left hind leg knocked by the car, which braked, but not quite in time. All members rushed out, including the children, each group blaming the other. 'Let's rush him to the vet's,' a tear for her child and concerned for the animal saviour, *Kakiji* was the first to act. Shekhar and Mina could clearly see the bordering-on-repentance and guilt expressions on their aunt's face.

On the way to the vet's, Geeta whispered to her brother, 'That's not something you see often. *Kakiji* is one of those with a golden heart, but you rarely see the gold shine on the exterior.' And sure enough, it was she who kept vigil for much of the evening, as the dog lay sedated. Everyone doted on the hero of the hour and until he was on his all fours, for he limped for quite some time after the incident. Needless to say, henceforth his popularity was universal.

As he got older there were hushed discussions between elders about neutering. Ali also had one of his first 'Adult' discussions with Shekhar and assured him, 'like many neighbourhood dogs, ours also has a girlfriend or two and if you look around, there are chances of spotting his miniature versions roaming about!'

As time went by, sure enough, just as Father had said all those years ago, as the children started growing up, their pet started growing old. Shekhar remarked to his guru, 'How disheartening it is to see man's best friend leaving him, just when he seems to need him most.'

'*Ni kweli*, *Kijana* (it's true, youngster), you won't find a better friend, animal or human, for that matter.' With his advancing years, they put him to pasture, replacing his guard duties with a young *Askari* (guard) not that he had ever caught any burglars, in reality being just one more member of the family. When he was finally no more, each and every one within the compound felt his absence, acknowledging they were minus one member of the household ...

Chapter 14

Monkey business

One weekend Ali returned from a long-delayed visit to his home town, the coastal village of Malindi, located approximately 70 miles north of Mombasa. What was different about this visit from the rest was that he had brought a friend with him, a monkey. Brown furred, beady, yellowish brown eyes with a small cute face and finally a long tail. This part of his anatomy stretched all the way down to his friend and benefactor Ali's knee, when he perched on top of his left shoulder, a favourite but rarely accessible location. The kids of the household went berserk with delight, bombarding Ali with all sorts of questions: 'where did you find him?', 'How old is he?', 'What's his name?' Simba, who was two at the time, initially apprehensive, with tail upright and hair on his ridge going edgy every time, became a chum as time went by.

Ali explained to the elders. 'He actually belongs to my brother but I've had to bring him here as the brother is away from home for a while.' Dad, perceptive as ever, smiled knowingly and said, 'I'm sure that's not the only reason. Your restless soul always tends to get involved in new "projects" every now and then, although you are invariably able to keep things under control. Well, he's your responsibility, so watch out for him.'

The children named him Micky, after one of the comic book characters. During the day, he was tied to a large tree which had several strong branches outside the compound in front of the garage. The leash was long, so the primate had enough mobility. He was fed, mostly by the child entourage on tropical fruits and nuts of which there was no dearth at the coast. At night Ali tied him just outside his quarters.

On the first evening as twilight approached, Ali called all the kids round to satisfy their curiosity and answer their questions. 'You can call him whatever you like but as to his roots, well my brother lives at a *shamba* (farm) at the edge of Malindi village and during one of his hunting expeditions in the forest beyond, he saw this monkey which seemed to have been separated from his mother and family members; they usually move and reside in groups. 'I have brought him with me until my *Ndugu* (brother) returns from his business trip.' Micky seemed happy enough in his new surroundings and enjoyed fooling about with the children.

Kakiji immediately had her comments, 'We've got enough chipmunks in the family,' referring to the human brood, 'without adding one more.' However, in matters where Ali was concerned, she would only protest so much and no more as she, like every member was aware of the man's indispensability in all matters, hence certain liberties were invariably allowed from time to time.

In the early evenings, with Micky perched on his shoulder, Ali along with Shekhar, Nilesh and Simba went for walks. When they reached suitable open ground or vegetation, the monkey was allowed movement, subject to the long leash that was specially prepared. For a while, everything seemed calm and trouble free. However, as the elders said, 'A monkey isn't a monkey, until and unless he performs his tricks.' Sure enough, one morning after the working members and elder children had left, there was a big noise in the kitchen. Osman had probably forgotten to secure the leash at the tree and Micky sensing his opportunity, went exploring. The first and obvious place was the kitchen.

The sound of smashing utensils caused Mum to rush from inside towards the kitchen. The workers were busy with laundry outside and they too ran in. The kitchen was in a mess, with broken glass, cutlery and other utensils sprawled on the floor. Micky, the culprit jumping all over the place, with banana in one hand and berries in the other, hopped out of the kitchen area and into the rear garden. Ali instructed his sidekick and they apprehended the mischief maker. As Ali explained later, 'We caught the *nugu* (monkey) just in the nick of time or else he might have jumped behind the rear (four foot) wall into the bushes.'

Needless to say, all the elders had something to say about the incident, but to keep it short, Dad warned the in-charge, 'One more incident and off he goes, wherever and however you may wish to dispose (of) him.'

Shekhar and the others found it amusing, of course, and exclaimed Nilesh, 'What a piece of bad luck, should have happened on a Saturday!' The older boys had bragged about their new pet to everyone at school and all the mates kept on asking to bring it along. 'At least bring him once,' some pleaded, 'or are you guys making up a story,' dared the more rowdy ones. So, taking up the mini challenge on the last day of term, with prior arrangement, the chauffeur/driver along with Osman brought Micky to the school after promising Ali that utmost care would be taken to avoid any mishaps. 'Any trouble of any sort and you all will be answerable to me,' Ali warned, as he could be stern when required.

Getting Micky used to the car was a problem, as, compared to a bus, he seemed to find it claustrophobic. Osman soon cooled him off and said, 'a steady supply of your favourite monkey(!) nuts if you behave,' and that did the trick. Nearly half their year's students gathered round to see the special guest at home time. The vendors selling peanuts, *papetas* (dry, acidic fruit) and other fruit, had a field day as everyone, boys as well as the girls, wanted to stroke and feed the primate and began to purchase the items. Nilesh took charge and stopped the over-feeding lest their little friend got ill or worse. Presently the Assistant Head got wind of the matter and his arrival caused a quick dispersal of the crowd. On their way home, the boys, rather pleased with themselves expressed, 'Well you seem to have had a grand time, little fellow and enjoyed all the fuss everyone made over you.'

'And without any trouble, too,' added Osman, who would have been answerable the most, had any occurred. A couple of weeks later, Ali brought the sad tidings that his brother was back home and that their young friend had to be returned. The kids were all heartbroken but there was nothing they could do. Shekhar, cousin Geeta and Nilesh wanted one last adventure with the chimp and on the final Saturday joined by the young kids they all went to town. This was the same Salim Road market where the boys had had their punishment a couple of years before. Whilst purchasing some fruit the little fellow toppled a few baskets and nearly caused a ruckus, but everything was controlled in the nick of time by the boys despite the *Mamas* throwing knowing glances. Nilesh joked with his cousin, 'perhaps some of them recognise us from before!'

When the day of parting came, the kids, sullen faced, all gave their final goodbyes, with Ali trying to cheer them up, 'We'll try and bring him back some day or maybe even pay a visit to Malindi to my *ndugu's shamba.'*

As the car sped away to take them to the bus stop in town, the kids stood outside for a long while. For several days afterwards the tree in the front was regularly visited, to remind them of their little friend who had stolen their tender little hearts and in the hope that they would see him again soon ...

Chapter 15

More school days!

By now, Shekhar and friends, who were due to enter High School, were 'getting the picture.' Life was less about play and fun and more about education and knowledge, disciplined physical development, acquiring social skills which included religious tolerance. At the coast they had, in addition to their Hinduism, Islam as well as the Ismaili faith under the Aga Khan, Christianity though applicable mostly to the colonials, and Sikhism. Nice cross-cultural learning about each other, provided you took the interest and of course adults had to play their part as well.

However, the biggest responsibility fell on the teacher, of course, the one who moulds the above virtues into the pupil. But then there are teachers ... and there are teachers ...

The Coast Indian Boys' High School was located halfway outside the boundary of Mombasa town. On the first day, the newcomers were taken round by the Head Prefect: 'We have the lower/junior forms at the bottom, higher at the top, science laboratories at the left precinct, and the library on the north side opening out onto the playing fields. Finally, there is the central assembly area backing onto the spacious school hall at the central lower precinct.'

Shekhar, not surprisingly and true to his family traits found his favourites to be the two English classes, language and literature. The second including of course,

Shakespeare, Bernard Shaw among others, as well as Gujarati, his mother tongue, since French or Latin as well as Swahili were introduced only after independence.

Extra-curricular activities like swimming, cricket and drama were the favourites.

The only real problem was mathematics, which he had never had a real aptitude for, and for that one had to accept the assistance of his mate Arif who possessed the quintessential Indian mind, which seems to have a knack for all forms of arithmetical dilemmas. Luckily most of his peers fell in this category so help was always at hand.

'Arif, I hereby and henceforth, proclaim thee my Mathematics Guru,' said the struggling student, only half in jest, to his pal, a whizz with numbers. 'Other categories of figures I can manage without your help, thank you, but logarithms ... simultaneous equations ... geometrical theorems ...' he sighed and placed his hand on his head in despair!

Lifelong friendships, some formed while in the junior school, continued. Dilip, whose family too were close to Shekhar's own, Arif, and last but not least Indrajit Singh, whose rare Punjabi humour and dialect was very popular. Rare, because most of the Sikh community abounded upcountry in Nairobi and other towns.

'I think we should consider ourselves lucky,' Shekhar said to Dilip one evening after cricket practice, 'Having such a close-knit friend circle (the 'gang of five' as it was always popularly known) and from such diverse cultures too. 'The other day I met my English/ Portuguese neighbour,' he continued. 'He studies at a boarding school upcountry at the town of Gilgil, and comes to Mombasa during his holidays.' (Unlike upcountry and at the highlands, there was some social intercourse between the colonials and other communities, albeit in the professional sector, at the coast.)

Shekhar reminisced the meeting and relayed it to his friend: It was a Saturday afternoon and I was in the garden chatting to Osman, our gardener when I heard sounds from the next door bungalow garden. A young white boy, about my own age was firing gun pellets towards trees growing beyond the safety wall. I noticed with dismay that a couple of pellets had already found their mark and two birds had fallen on the ground. Being a budding conservationist and lover of all things in nature, as you well know, I could not just let things be. I stood by the hedge and after our greetings, we chatted for a while about boys' interests in general, 'By the way, you're pretty good with that shooter,' I said to him, not to start on the wrong footing.

'Thanks, I got the gun for my last birthday,' said my neighbour, beaming with pride at the compliment as well as the miniature toy weapon in his hand.

'Why don't you try something different? Put the gun away and take this.' I went inside and came out with some seeds and bread pieces which the mums always fed *their* birds with. After a cat got one of them Ali had made a makeshift feed box to be placed on a thin tree branch. I went over from a hedge gap and gave some to the boy and placed the rest on the ground. We watched from a distance.

For a long while nothing happened, but just when the host was on the point of irritation, they came. First one, then two and finally a whole chirping brood. When they finished and flew away, I inquired of my hopefully new found friend, 'Tell me, which gave you more of a thrill, blowing their poor brains out, or this?' I pointed to the ground.

'My neighbour did not answer for a while. Then he smiled, just half a smile it was, but something seemed to stir inside him.'

'By the way I'm James,' he said suddenly. I responded likewise.

'Look, I've got to go now,' he said, but why don't you come home sometime, say next Sunday evening, we're having a small party, my younger brother and I?'

I thanked him and we parted. Just before entering house, I glanced furtively across the hedge.

'James was still standing in his doorway, and still looking at the weapon that he held in his hand.'

The raconteur paused.

'Well, what happened then?' Dilip was getting impatient.

'Oh nothing much, we've been friends ever since; his mum is most kind, and as for the gun, I haven't seen or heard it much since, except for some target practice,' smiled Shekhar to his pal, as he finished his little tale.

The schooling and discipline at C.I.B.H. was strict generally, moulded after the British education system, and to implement it there was an English Headmaster and a couple of English teachers too. One hundred plus lines, runs around the track and six of the best or worse, as a last resort were some of the punishments, which after the first couple of years became less frequent except for only the greediest!

As at the primary school, there were various breeds of teacher. Mr Mehta taught history and P.E. or P.T. (physical education/training). Lean, fairly muscular and tall, he sported a thick moustache. His conduct was both friendly, and considering his loud delivery, at times intimidating.

Shekhar, was tempted mischievously on occasion to ask whether he had ever been in the armed forces but somehow never got a 'suitable' opportunity. Overall, though, one could say that under the tough, army-like appearance, beat a humane, fairly compassionate heart and even though in his anger he let out a few 'unkind' words or phrases the students did not take him too seriously. Being a history teacher, he was fond of comparing the occasionally badly behaved students, or making references, to historical characters, one of them being the comical Spanish protagonist Don Quixote. 'Stop EN-TER-TAINING yourself with delusions of grandeur, Senior Don, and get on with the work,' he would often say, shaking his head simultaneously. A favourite line upon displeasure was 'YOU are a *strange* idiot?!' (one would have thought, most idiots would be strange to start with!)

Whenever he dictated notes, loudly of course, either due to the sheer enjoyment or revelry of it or perhaps because he forgot his lines, one of his favourite words became the conjunction 'and.' After every few words he would pause and emphatically say 'and,' with the students looking up to see what was coming next, and sure enough once again 'and' then finally a last quick one before finally finding his lines, which would be something like (for the fourth time) 'and ... the Explorer Vasco Da Gama reached the Cape of Good Hope,' upon which sighed the thankful pupils, uttering, '*and* – at last *ringeth* the bell,' signifying the end of the history lesson!!

Then there was Mrs Daruwala, quite possibly many a senior schoolboys' fantasy. Pretty, with almond-like brown eyes, above average in height and having a fantastic dress sense. One would not exactly refer to her as a Madhubala (the '50s Indian pin-up girl and more), but she was no doubt attractive enough in her own way. Keeping in mind the hot weather, it was silk sarees and Punjabi dresses and with her spry, almost rhythmic way of walking complete with high-heeled shoes, the lady invariably distracted the attention of male teachers and senior students alike, setting aflutter many a pining heart!

As for her teaching, you could not complain here either. English literature for the final year was her class and not being averse to the subject both Indrajeet and Shekhar were among her favourites.

'A pity indeed,' teased Dilip and the others frequently,

(referring to one of their literature texts, Bernard Shaw's *Caesar and Cleopatra*) 'that neither of our gallant heroes, despite Cleopatra's ever presence, qualifies, as a Caesar ... or for that matter, a Mark Anthony!'

Mr Jones, English, by birth was as near-perfect a specimen of a teacher you would hope to find. He had spent some years in India during the Raj and had adapted himself well to most things Indian and now African too. Well-dressed, and well-spoken, with a kind demeanour, here was a teacher who, indeed, did his profession proud, and that was an understatement.

A staunch believer in the aphorism 'there is no such thing as a bad boy.' Mr Jones, in his (English Language) class, treated 15 year olds as adults, with the result that he had, on only the most isolated of incidents needed to castigate a student.

There were rumours among teachers that he had had to leave an (Indian) lady love behind on the sub-continent, due to social constraints and subsequently had remained a bachelor. Thus, although he was quite open about most matters, when questioned about his younger days by his concerned students, he would reply, beginning in archetypal English fashion, 'Listen old chap or Mister so and so, *Sasa Kenya ni inchi yangu, nyinyi ni watu yangu*' (Kenya is now my country and you are my people) ... thereby ending further discussion on the subject.

On the last day of the final year the students held a special goodbye with individual speeches planned. However, such was the throat-lumping emotion in all their hearts, that only the briefest of lines emanated. 'Whatever you have taught us, Sir, shall remain with us always as shall your memory, wherever we go, whatever we do, and you may rest assured, Sir, we shall never let you down ...'

Mr Jones was visibly moved and as for his boys ...

there was probably not a single dry eye in the house.

Lastly we come to the science teacher, Mr Sheikh, the Bull – so-called by the students due to his partiality to the expression 'bull shit,' modified sometimes to 'shit of a bull.' Whenever he disagreed with a student – which was most of the time – that was the expression you were likely to hear. In fact, he did not look very unlike a bull himself. Of stocky build, curly hair and a broad, tight fisted walk, as if he owned the school and what was within its four walls. For most students thus, Mr Sheikh wasn't exactly flavour of the month and when he began crossing limits, even by his standards which included heavy detentions and excessive assignments, it was decided, unanimously by senior class 3b (inhabited, of course, by most members of the 'gang of five') to do something about it.

Stink bombs and fire crackers ...

The morning assembly on the day, was as usual at 8 a.m. sharp. A science project had gone very well and Mr Sheikh was to be commended in the assembly by the Headmaster at ten past.

Precisely at 8.12 a.m., according to a previous plan (which was supported by all but a few model students, Shekhar being one of them, of course), the fire crackers went off. Planted by 'experts' in the lobby which joined the left with the right, and directly opposite the assembly area. The Headmaster's face went redder than the crackers themselves ...

'I want the culprits apprehended at all costs,' said Mr Madigan. However, nothing broke the solidarity of those involved despite persuasion or threats. Mr Sheikh was, as required, furious and marched off soon to his first class of the day, chemistry.

What greeted him as well as the students here was

less noisy but nastier. Stink bombs had been released!! The 'Bull' just stood in front of the class, all students covering their faces with smarting eyes and for a while they felt he would let himself loose in the arena of the lab class and charge at all and sundry, but instead he bellowed: 'Keep standing, all of you and for the full 45 minutes unless you tell me who the hell is responsible for this.' The reply was, of course total silence.

Subsequent to this double debacle, the nasty Mr Sheikh appeared sufficiently tamed, especially as the Head also had come to know of his misdemeanours.

Henceforth he managed to keep a somewhat lower profile.

Chapter 16

All in a day's ... Cricket!

For nearly every Asian youngster Cricket was *Numero uno* on their sports list as, to a large extent, it still remains. Shekhar and friends were no exception. Despite substantial practice after school hours, weekends too were often spent with oak and willow ...

It was Saturday and it was hot. The thermometer had reached 100 Fahrenheit. Shekhar had just put on his cricket whites and was on his way to pick up Dilip and Arif. The heat was so intense and sticky, one wished to go into an ice-filled tub no sooner than one had taken a shower and changed into gear. For those in school, weekends meant cricket and more cricket, with the elders having to slog in offices at least on Saturday mornings. The grounds, Ismaili Gymkhanas, Sikh Unions or Patel clubs were all in action. Then of course there were the inter-school matches and this team was playing against Aga Khan High School today.

'I'd like you to open with Laamba (the tall one, as the other star batter, Mukesh was nicknamed), as usual,' Dilip captaining, said to Shekhar as he entered his VW Beetle, a recent present from *Kakaji*, who liked to spoil his nephew now and then. 'I hope *Mote* (Fatty) is in form, his spin is going to be crucial.'

'Well, just don't challenge him (referring to his girth) into running the pitch at a go when he bats,' laughed Shekhar.

Arif was an all-rounder, Shekhar, given his stylish batting was, nevertheless, along with Dilip, into the game equally for the camaraderie but the real star was the gangly Ashok, who believed in boundaries and little else. Where others took singles, he would take 2s or even 3s, although sometimes to his detriment.

Having collected first Arif from the more affluent Nyali and now Dilip from the edge of town centre they made their way to the Gymkhana ground.

'Sometimes, methinks skipping a match on Saturday would not go amiss, what sayest thee, comrades?' asked Arif (who fancied himself a Hamlet or Othello, from time to time, English literature being his favourite after his earlier rejection, ever since Mrs Daruwala took over the class). He was of course referring in context to the young ladies in their maxis, bobbed hairdos and sunglasses all out in their Saturday best. The more conservative ladies were in their floral sarees, all worn modestly high, compared to the hipster versions yet to come. The men even more simply dressed, in their plain as well as bush shirts and loose, pleated and upturned trousers; cream suits and colourful ties for the more formal.

They briefly passed by Standard, Barclays and Ottoman (Banks), colonial stores, including the odd hunting equippers and taxidermists. Then there were the hotels, including the Castle hotel one of the oldest and most prominent built between the wars.

Finally, the cars: British made simple Ford Zephyrs, Consuls and Prefects contrasting with the flamboyant American Limousines, pink, turquoise and cream, some with their half-hidden wheels, others with their expanded fins and occasional convertibles too. In between came the toughies or dust biters for safari, the French Peugeots, German Mercs and of course the ubiquitous Beetle.

Street vendors selling mangoes, *madafu* and Victoria fruit, and Arabs clinking their porcelain cups and saucers selling *kahawa.*

Both the team members knew each other quite well through cricket and other activities. Today, though, Shekhar's team were spitting blood. 'We have to avenge the previous match defeat at all costs,' said the captain. 'Just look at the ground, it's packed. A lot of supporters have arrived and crucially, there are girl cheerleaders present for both our sides. It's a question of honour!'

The ground was quite large, by school standards, and the spectator area was full to the brim. It had rained the previous night and when the guest team won the toss they took advantage of the ground conditions and decided to bowl first. When Mukund ('Fatty') hurt himself halfway, Dilip took three successive star wickets turning the match in the visitors' favour. At half-time Shekhar asked him in the changing room, customarily *'Bona una cheza kama risasi. Lazima ni wanawake, sio?'* (How come you've played like gunfire? Must be the girls, right?)

The reply, of course, was just silence, a smirk.

In any event, the opponents had set a comfortable target and the 'guests' had their revenge especially after *Laamba* hit numerous boundaries and managed a massive score, much to the delight, particularly of the female supporters.

Champagne was smuggled in by one of the winning team mates. (Twenty-one was the legal limit and these chaps were hardly 18!)

After a match, it was customary to (make) 'camp' at one of the mates' places for tea and a post-mortem of the preceding event and today it was Mukund's turn. When his mother served up her speciality, her *bhajias* (the variety was limitless, onion, chilly, potato, brinjal, you name it), Arif could not control his flattery, *'Mummyji,* your *bhajias* easily rival Mombasa's best bhajia houses any day. Let's open our own restaurant; you be the chef and *mimi nita chunga biashara* (... I will control the finances).'

After washing them down with Coke which was now rivalling the original Pepsi, the friends moved to the living room, the furniture of which was adorned with serious literature in one section and leisure reading on the other. Various comic books were lying in a heap. In a corner was a gramophone player with a whole stack of Vinyl 78rpm records. Most of these were Indian film tracks and although many of the gang were more into Western rock and roll music, the host loaded one record for his guests' pleasure, saying, 'You won't have heard a song like this.'

It was a recently released track from a forthcoming Indian film, a cricket song, albeit not without romantic connotations and the lyrics went something like this:

> *She ney khela He sey aaj* Cricket Match*! (wow wow)*
> *Ek nazar mein dil bechara ho gaya L.B.W.!*' (wow wow) ...
>
> ... *Usney phenka* Legbreak *tao humne mara chhakka!* Out *karta kaun hamey hum khiladi Pukka!*
>
> *Armanon ki* Crease *sey badh gaye hum to agey aur uski chal dekh kar, kar diye hakka bukka!*
>
> Cricket *men to jeet gaye par harey pyar ka* Match *(wow wow)* ...
>
> ... *Ek nazar mein dil bechara ... ho ... gaya ... L ... B ... W ...!*

The poet writes here for aspiring Romeos, fusing cricket terminology with the romantic:

> '*The she(s) have played with the he(s) today, a Cricket match*
> *It has taken but one gaze for the poor heart to go L.B.W.!*
> *The (opposition) has thrown a leg break and we have hit a* chhakka *(sixer)!*
> *Who would dare to get us 'out' we are players Pukka!*

*We have overstepped the 'Crease' (limit) of our
aspirations and their (presumably intoxicating/
sexy) stride has caused us to to go in a total daze!
Cricket we have managed to win, but lost the game
of love ...*
*... It has taken but one gaze for the poor heart to go
L.B.W. ...*

"Well next time we play a match, said Arif, we ought to
sing the song at the game, the girls will love it!'

It was perhaps the only Indian song on the game and
of course became a cult hit.

The last phase of the day was still not over and the
members debated. 'Still have time to paint the town red,
any suggestions, chaps?' posed Shekhar. 'Well, there's
no party planned, so it'll have to be a takeaway followed
by *John Wayne*,' answered a couple of the gang. So, a
few quick showers later, all ventured into the fresher
evening air. Dusk was approaching and although the
customary droplets of sweat began their slow run from
foreheads, the cool breeze gave it a pleasant icy feel.

The Indian radio stations, via the residences plus the
occasional street transistors relayed song numbers on
sanjh ki bela (evening hour/time).

The VW Beetle roared towards town and Salim Road
and after a quick take away, they queued for the Duke's
latest at the Regal, their favourite cinema haunt, for the
'last picture show'. It was nearly midnight as they
walked back to the car. The streets were still bustling
with traffic and the mostly – adult – public and a few in
their late teens.

The beat of the surf waves was mildly audible to him
as Shekhar, having reached home, walked past the rear
garden. Changing into night gear he was just flopping
into bed when cousin Nilesh, momentarily woken from
his slumber, one eye open, inquired 'It's past midnight,
what have you been up to?' 'Oh, just messing about with
some cricket,' Shekhar answered, barely hearing his

own reply as he made his way into dreamland ...

Chapter 17

Navratri ... Diwali ... and all that hype!

Of all the festivals listed in the Indian calendar, the Navratri, followed a month later by the Diwali or Dipawali, are the most colourful and also the most revered in East Africa, as everywhere else where the Indian resides, celebrations have invariably been performed with the same zealous devotion, enthusiasm and joy as on the sub-continent. This particular year, the family would have relatives from western Kenya as well as Uganda (during Navratri).

'I've been asking your *Jeeja ji*, Sudha and the kids to visit (brother-in-law Ashok and Shekhar's maternal aunt Sudha lived in Nakuru) and they've at last confirmed they are driving down to Mombasa,' confirmed Dad a week before to Shantaben (Mum).

'They haven't seen some of the toddlers and of course, there is the additional attraction,' smiled Dad at his darling daughter. Geeta, younger to Shekhar by a couple of years, celebrated her birthday during these auspicious days.

The hype in the Vakil home at times occasionally extended to hysteria among the ladies and younger female members what with the hot weather, impending arrival of guests and the event, plus all that colourful dressing, not to speak of the mini birthday celebration in between. The male members especially the juniors were excited too, they hadn't met their counterparts for some time. Travel between the three East African Territories was done by car and rail during those days and hence not so frequent.

On the first evening, venues all over town were filled with people, participants, musicians as well as spectators, the elderly who had had their dancing days and now watched the next generations with blessings apparent. One of the most popular *Garba* (dance) played on 'poonam', the tenth night during those days was:

Taliyo na taley ... Taliyo na taley, Gori Garbe ghoomi gaye re ...

Poonam ni Raat oogi, Poonam ni Raat ...

Aasmani ... Aasmani Odhnina Odhania leheray re ...

Poonam ni raat oogi, Poonam ni raat ...

(rough translation:)

To the rhythm of (tuneful) clapping, do the maidens perform the *Garba* (Dance),

The night of the full moon has arrived, the night of the full moon ...

(Sky) Blue head-scarves sway away,

The night of the full moon has arrived, the night of the full moon ...

Towards the climax, when faster tunes and rhythms were required, musicians invariably played one of the public's favourites, the *Been* (Indian Clarinet) tune from the film song number, '*mann doley meira tann doley*'. The film (*Nagin*) and the song had been released just a couple of years before and was an absolute rage. (Amazingly it is still played at Navratri festivals today after all these decades, the only difference being, the harmonium has been substituted with the electric keyboard organ!)

Their own community being rather a small one, the family normally attended one of the larger community halls, the '*Patel Samaj*' (Patel community) was one particular preference. The gents in the family attended some nights, but the ladies wouldn't miss a single night for anything. Showing off (some of them!) their impressive and glittering saree collections and meeting up with some old acquaintances not seen for a while, in addition to the main, religious interest.

Shekhar and friends participated occasionally as they were still into western music, to a fair extent. For the male/youth in addition to the musical fanfare and dance, 'girl-watching' was the other attraction. As mentioned earlier, close contact was rare in those days unless the one you fancied happened to be your sister's best friend's cousin's sister, or thereabouts!

Nilesh observed, 'Funny, isn't it, the male dance is referred to as the female-sounding *Garbi* whereas it's the *Garba* for the ladies!!'

When they were very young, the children were enlightened with tales from Indian mythology by *Kakiji*, an obvious expert on all cultural matters. 'The *Navratri* (nine nights) have been celebrated four times a year from the earliest times but the most important one precedes Diwali (certain communities in northern India celebrate in April, alone). Additionally, the *Sharad Poonam* (night of the full moon) is the tenth night normally falling around the fifteenth day of the month. The festival is a homage to the deity, Mother Amba who protected her celebrants in the old days from evil in various ways, as she does at present to those who believe. The celebrations represent the various forms of blessings bestowed, including good health, wealth, and happiness.'

On the tenth night after the *Aarti* (prayers), Geeta's closest friends announced her birthday and once the *Garba* celebrations had ended, the entourage moved to the Vakil residence where the birthday celebrations awaited.

As usual Ali and co had taken charge of things. The tables had been laid out in the garden leaving the central area empty for more dance activity which in the event would be the *Dandias*.

The full moon in all its splendour and glory looked down upon the revellers, with the slightly audible sound of the surf on the not so distant beach below, as well as the Nyali Bridge and Nyali residence appeared in their faint lighting.

The adults relaxed in the laid-out arm-chairs and Dad spoke on behalf of all: 'How wonderful to see all these youngsters together after all this time. You must come to the coast more often, Ashokbhai.'

Finally, the tired youngsters awaited the final event: cake cutting and dinner.

'Count the candles,' shouted the boys as Geeta blew them.

By the time dinner was served and finished it was almost midnight and it was time to say their good-nights. 'Bye, Birthday Girl,' shouted the departing friends in chorus as the last remnants of the event were cleared and everyone prepared for slumber ...

Diwali (Dipawali)

This, the main and most auspicious, could be said to be the Indian equivalent of Christmas.

According to Indian mythology, the first such celebration took place when Lord Ram defeated Ravan, the ten-headed monster king of Lanka (now Sri Lanka).

Sita, the consort of Lord Ram had been abducted by Ravan when Ram and his brother Laxman were in exile Lord Ram with the help of the monkey god Hanuman, raised an army to rescue Sita and kill Ravan before returning to the northern city of Ayodhya.

The word *Dipawali* means an array of lights, which were first displayed apparently on arrival home by the victors, and this is followed by the *Naya Saal* or new year.

At last the big day arrived. The mood and the hype would continue for several days. The blasts of fire crackers, the food, the new clothes, and the gatherings.

'The shops are going to have a ball and do bumper business this year too,' said *Kakaji* to the family. This would include the Indian hotels working extra time with their orders of various sweetmeats, the drapers with the demand of sarees, children's clothing and the shops selling fire crackers, notwithstanding that they had only a few weeks earlier been busy with *Navratri*.

Shekhar, Nilesh and mates made their 'plans,' meaning controlled mischief. 'This year there is going to be gang warfare on a much bigger scale than the last two years, I hear,' said Mukesh, who always seemed to obtain this kind of news very quickly and accurately through his informants. This meant that the nasty ones would throw their ammunition at moving vehicles, ladies and opposition gangs.

There were other victims too, the poor pets (dogs) who invariably hid under beds or other safe areas and the native African children who had crackers thrown around their resident quarters.

'We will try to steer clear of these lot, as we don't want a repetition of last year when we got carried away somewhat and had a long lecture from our elders,' said Shekhar.

The women folk had been busy too as expected. Although not everyone is a fan of the Diwali edibles like the *ghoogras* (sweet *soji/semolina,* shell shaped) and *mathias* (crispy, spicy puffs) fried on a large scale in many *Gujarati* homes – depending upon size, tradition somehow gets the better of things and they invariably turn up at teatime during the festive days, (with the more popular *Chevda*).

Some schools had half-days, others a holiday and the

families went to the temple.

'Wow,' was the sound that emanated from the twins, when they saw the vast variety and quantity of sweets on offer to the deities. 'Mum, I've never seen so many sweet items at one place,' exclaimed Radha.

'The primary idea is to show devotion to the deities, not for you lot to scoff all that sugary stuff,' laughed her elder cousin Geeta.

In the evening, 'gang warfare' was in full swing at every nook and cranny and the members made full use of their 'artillery' to let off steam which had built up during the preceding twelve months following their defeat or victory whatever the case maybe at their last encounter.

The nasty ones did not stop there of course and they had a grand if sadistic time harassing the ladies throwing the mini bombs at their silk sarees. The ones apprehended were taught a lesson by the police and authorities, never to be forgotten. And there were less harmful pursuits as in the case of Nilesh, Shekhar and co, who frightened pets and native children from a distance and more inventively or innovatively blasted noisy 'bombs' under bridges which gave a resoundingly loud echo much to the bewilderment and fear of drivers above!!

The 'rockets' were, along with the noisy 'blasters' the most popular items. When the last of these were blasted off into the starry night above, Nilesh suddenly remembered what he had seen in the media and joked, 'I wonder if poor *Layka* is still in orbit and able to see our earthly frolics

Yes. the Russians had then recently sent this female dog in their first space venture. After a grand cracker- or cracking-party the youngsters made homeward bound. The next day was *Naya Saal* or the Indian new year according to the Hindu calendar.

Ali and Osman started work early and wished '*Saal Mubarak*' (happy new year) to all family members.

The custom was to visit close friends and relations at their homes which was reciprocated during the day. Others were met at common venues like temples and centres. The normal offering was nuts and dry fruits ...

Chapter 18

The illusions of first love ... the pain ... and the whole damn thing!

It was beginning of the third year. Shekhar and a couple of friends had been invited to a birthday party of a senior student, they were well known to.

'Do you know, Nalin's is considered one of the most affluent and influential families in Mombasa's social circles,' commented Arif as they were being driven to the party by an elder. 'They live in what is probably considered to be the best locality of the island next to Nyali Beach and wait till you see the house!'

Upon arrival Nalin conducted introductions. 'Meet my sister Rita,' he said to his latest guests.

So far, none of the mates had taken a serious interest in any particular member of the opposite sex. Teasing and whistling were the occasional pastimes of the naughtier ones but Shekhar's style was the more sober approach, if and when the situation arrived.

'Pleased to meet you, Rita,' was the reaction, however the feeling was one of delight, rather than just pleasure. If ever there was a girl who had taken his fancy it was this smart, rather vivacious looker, dressed in a maxi and matching top, adorning a bobbed hairstyle flashing an illuminating, confident, almost arrogant smile.

It was a balmy, pleasantly warm night, rare for the otherwise humid coast and to the tune of the portable gramophone, the youngsters began dancing the night away. Despite himself, Shekhar was intrigued by this girl, who was clearly a year or two older than his approaching sixteen years, and for whom he now had to wait a while for his turn to ask for a dance. The only elders were the host's parents and immediate family who watched the youngsters with interest. Nalin's father commented to a family elder, 'It looks like Elvis Presley, and others like him have turned rock and roll into a religion for our teenagers, at least those exposed to western music and culture.'

With a laugh, commented the other, 'Well, as long as they do not forsake their own culture and art!'

During the jive, Rita's eyes did not waiver from her partner nor did her special smile diminish. Later they talked on many subjects. 'Nalin tells me you are a guy with not a few talents, referring to Shekhar's prowess at drama, debate, in addition to some sport; and you dance as well!' she said only half mockingly.

'Oh, the last one depends on the partner,' smiled the recipient. 'By the way, I didn't know Nalin had such a smart sister; mind you he and I don't meet that often during school, it's more on the sports field.'

Finally, aware of her age advantage she became more open in her talk and joked, 'What a shame, I can't seem to bump into anybody nice my age!'

Shekhar defended with, 'Oh I'm sure there isn't that much ...' but Rita had moved away, waving to someone at the far corner. For a while, the young man pondered on whether the girl was just teasing or being serious.

Arif came over presently. 'I noticed you've joined the queue,' and upon seeing the apparent bewilderment on his pal's face he continued ... 'of the lady's admirers' ...

'A word of advice,' continued his bosom buddy. 'Enough tender hearts have been broken, and fingers burned ... you're too clever to be one of those.'

'She sure is something,' was the only reply that emanated from the somewhat dazed youngster, who hardly appeared to have heard his friend.

Further introductions and conversation took place, but Shekhar's eyes kept on searching for the young lady who had cast the die and then suddenly disappeared from sight momentarily, then re-appeared laughing and chatting to some other potential victim, if her reputation, according to Arif was to be believed.

It was getting late and they left soon after.

A few days passed before Shekhar made up his mind. He had to see the girl. More warnings had come from friends, 'She's no good ... only interested in fooling around' and 'The spoilt daughter of a rich father ... keep away from her,' said a drama buddy. However, the arrogant, challenging demeanour was hard to resist and against his better judgement one afternoon after school the smitten lad made his way to the girls' high school at finishing time.

They bumped at some distance from the gates, and after exchanging greetings she offered him a lift in her chauffeur-driven Limousine. Shekhar after initial refusal accepted, for that was the idea. 'You disappeared the other evening at your party,' he said in a complaining tone.

'Oh, I'm sorry, there were so many guests and some I hadn't met for ages.'

Once again, she was all smile and charm and just before alighting at a convenient bus stop, Shekhar asked, 'How about meeting at Rosa's tomorrow, it's Saturday.' Rosa's was an extremely popular cafe haunt for teenagers especially on Saturdays while in town.

'By the way, you **are** aware of our age difference, I hope,' she said, with half a smile.

'Yes, but does it bother you? It doesn't bother me in the least,' was the instant response.

Rita didn't reply, but instead paused for a moment and said, 'I'll see you at eleven.' Then, impulsively biting her lower lip, she slapped him gently on the cheek just before the car moved off.

They met on the Saturday as planned. The place was packed and noisy. Sometimes it was frequented after the Saturday morning picture show at noon. Ice cream sodas, samosas and other specialities were in full swing and demand.

Shekhar was on the dot, but Rita came after 10 minutes. 'Sorry I'm late,' she smiled. Everyone was looking their way, including previous rejects. They talked for quite a while and then departed.

There were a couple of further meetings, as the lady admired some of Shekhar's special qualities, restraint being one of them. However, the young man was waiting for the right moment and at an intimate one at a discreet restaurant, despite her initial denials, Shekhar managed to 'steal' a couple of passionate kisses which she ultimately surrendered to. They last met at a mutual friend's wedding. Rita looked a smash in her heavy and colourful Sari.

'Someday you'll be sitting in that *Mandap*,' joked Shekhar, waiting to see her reaction.

'Oh yeah, with the right groom partner,' she responded immediately, not being outdone.

Soon, it was the end of the year and as she had warned she left for further studies to the sub-continent. In a surprise – but not unwanted – phone call on the last day she promised to keep in touch. The initial semi-intimate letters then became less and less frequent.

Shekhar confided to pal Dilip, 'I know what you're going to say, but it's most beguiling. First she promises to write on her own accord and then suddenly dwindles off.'

His mate gave a knowing look and hunched his shoulders.

A few months later Shekhar heard Rita was in town for holidays. He waited for a call which did not come and on the first Saturday after, he happened to see her in town. She was in a Limousine driven by a young man along with what was obviously a group of friends.

Shekhar called and waived; the lady obviously recognised but refused to acknowledge and just drove off with her entourage.

For the first time in his life the young man experienced betrayal, hurt, insult. It was as if he had been slapped in front of all eyes watching.

That evening the 'gang' members had a meeting at Dilip's. His *Kanu mama* (maternal uncle) whom everybody among the younger generation referred to simply as *Mamaji* came to the rescue as Dilip had briefed him earlier.

'There is only one person we can turn to for sorting out 'special', domestic and other social problems as you know, *Mamaji* and that is you.'

When a friend of Dilip's dad had a tiff with his other half, having him turn to alcohol and other consolations, it was this peacemaker who patched things up. Having moved to this continent in the earlier part of the twentieth century and spent quite a few years in the interior or 'bush' as it was referred to, he knew most of the native dialects and was often teased both by his men friends as well as the youngsters about his supposed first 'native' wife he had tucked away in some village.

'Young man, this is just the beginning, you are likely to meet quite a few ladies in your time. Don't take it too much to heart,' the elder consoled.

'Well, it wasn't as if I had delusions of *marrying* her someday, but the way she just ... Well I suppose I was warned by many.'

Somebody in the group then revealed, 'The guy she drives around with is a fabulously rich party and it seems a wedding is in the offing.'

Finally, to ease things *Mamaji* rounded off, 'You guys are taking this so seriously, think of those genuine love birds who are not allowed to pair, in spite of their sincere love for one another.' He cited two examples where couples from different communities, due to their parents' age-old, ultra-conservative ideas and double standards, were married to their parents' choice of partners. 'Can you think of anything more heartless? It would seem a harsh thing to say, but parents deservedly are only brought to their senses in many instances when girls commit suicide.'

'So, my boys, in matters of the heart, weigh things properly, and if you do fall in love – genuine love that is – make sure you are ready for hell and high water if necessary against daddy and/or mummy and the *samaaj*' (community).

With that, a somewhat pacified Shekhar and his mates thanked their elder friend and parted for the evening.

It was quite a while before the young man overcame the jilt although he did not allow himself to be weighed down by it. He managed to remove the girl 'out of his system' as the expression went. However, he would definitely henceforth view the opposite gender with a sharper outlook ...

Chapter 19

Maasai ... Man Eaters ... and Mzima Springs

School was out and Shekhar was getting bored. For a while he attended Dad's law firm, but then grew restless, the memories of the 'heartbreak' of his first romance also were relatively fresh. Arif, his close friend, had relations in Nairobi and he had been spending time with them.

One Sunday morning, much to his delight, Shekhar received an invitation from his friend to join him in Nairobi. Packing his bags, he was on his way to the capital within a couple of days, courtesy of East African Railways. Arif, who was staying with his uncle, Bashir, was waiting on the railway platform to receive him, along with the chauffeur. On their way home the former had a sneer on his face as he asked, 'Ever been on a jungle safari, I mean a real safari, Shekhu?'

'Why, no,' responded his mate.

'Well get set then, because that's what we're going to be up to, in a few days' time.'

Shekhar, quite excited, nevertheless, did not express himself as such, for he was busy observing the capital city from the window of their Impala Limousine. In the days before the oil crisis, most 'Big Shots' in the territories owned American cars and Chevrolets, Cadillacs, Buicks and Impalas were a common sight, with the Mercedes Benz following in second place.

After the heat and humidity of the coast, Nairobi, considered part of the highlands, seemed much cooler,

despite it being 'summertime.' They arrived at the suburban home at Parklands, which in those days was
extensively resided in by the Asian, with the more
exclusive suburbs of Muthaiga, Westlands, Karen and
Hurlingham still *wazungu* domain. The large style bungalow seems to be very popular in the tropics and this
one had the standard five bedrooms, along with open-
plan living room plus an annexe which served as a
relaxation/ smoking lounge. The table in the middle
clearly suggested the hosts used the room for playing
Bridge.

Outside at the front, a huge area for cars plus garden
and at the rear, further parking and servants' quarters.
Two large German-Shepherds came to greet the new
guest. This was conspicuous as, unlike on the coast,
break-ins were more rampant here.

The artiste in Shekhar admired the garden which
teemed with roses, the white and fragrant 'Queen of the
night,' the red hibiscus, the lavender and white flowered
shrub yesterday-today-tomorrow plus a couple of
jacaranda/blue-bell trees and finally the orange coloured 'golden showers,' the fallen flowers of which,
carpeted a large part of the garden floor.

After a light meal, siesta came quickly after the journey and it was only the uncle's arrival that woke the
guest.

The family was introduced over dinner. Uncle Bashir
turned out to be exceedingly charming and gregarious.
He was in his late thirties, six-foot, lean, pencil-mous-
tached, brown-eyed and even fairer in complexion than
many in his Ismaili community. In fact, with the impeccable English that he articulated, Shekhar felt, for a
moment, he was being introduced to an English acquaintance! There was Aunt Najma, the kind, motherly
hostess who looked after the guest's every requirement,
and a couple of children.

Over coffee in the lounge, Uncle Bashir spoke. 'I don't know how much Arif has briefed you, but I've got this friend – he is in the hunting business – whom I'm planning to accompany to the south around the Tsavo National Park, the largest stronghold of big game in Kenya. The Game Department has asked him to get rid of a couple of marauding lions; actually, they've attacked humans recently. Obviously, we are not part of the "hunting party" but we'll be accompanying him separately in our vehicle. I have been asking Johnston for ages what it feels like to stay, hunt and explore real bush country, particularly among the Maasai or other tribes and this is our chance. Also, we ought to get an opportunity with our "tour guide" to see some of the fauna/flora which are not easily accessible.'

In the pre-conservation days, hunting expeditions were the 'sport' of the elite colonials and tourists including Hollywood film people and other celebrities and camera-shooting safaris only gained popularity in later years, after the war as did the creation of national parks but not before the animal population was reduced indiscriminately. Sadly, a different type of hunting still persists; poaching of elephant for ivory (artefacts) and the Rhino for the horn – for its supposedly aphrodisiac properties.

The elder paused, and lit a cigarette. 'So, what do you say, young man, are you "game"?' He smiled at the pun.

'Absolutely,' said his young listener, all ears and alternately looking at his friend.

'Well, it's all settled then, we'll leave at the crack of dawn tomorrow.'

The sun was just breaking through the clouds; it was going to be a warm day as the party loaded their gear. Their steer for the adventure, Philip Johnston, was more or less what Shekhar expected him to be; above average in height, keen blue eyes, beefy build and a matching rough, gravelly voice, attired in bush shirt and half pants. They took the Nairobi-Mombasa roadway. At the time it was un-tarmacked which made it even more of an authentic safari. There were two vehicles, the hunter's Land Rover and Uncle Bashir's roomy Ford station wagon. They would be away for approximately four to five days thus in addition to the hunting gear, tent equipment, cooking items, suitable bush country clothing and various canned food items were loaded.

They made their way via Embakasi and Athi River to the small town of Machakos about 35 miles from the capital, where they were to pick up Johnston's 'sidekick' the Kamba tribesman, Mutiso. They passed the township and waited at an agreed site just outside it.

'Why such an early stoppage?' asked Uncle Bashir, as they all alighted from their vehicle.

The seeker smiled and elucidated, 'We are collecting our fifth member. Mutiso has accompanied me on my various hunting quests and I have yet to come against a better bow and arrow marksman in all my years; he has saved my life on more than one occasion.' Johnston continued, 'My man's forefathers originated from western Tanzania and settled in central to eastern Kenya including the Tsavo region which we are going to visit, later shifting to the less arid parts like Machakos here and Embu. Being good hunters as well as fighters, their traditional weapons being the *mshaali* (arrow) and the small 21 inch Kamba sword, they participated in elephant ivory poaching at the turn of the century and later they ended up fighting for the British during the two wars, initially conscripted as forced labour, but later joined due to economic necessity. Although famously known as 'soldiers of the queen' even after the wars, there is clear evidence of their participation and having taken the notorious '*thenge*' oath in the *mau*

mau rebellion along with the main, Kikuyu tribe.'

He paused briefly. 'Anyway all that is in the past, and although a new freedom fighter organisation calling itself the land freedom army has sprung up, the security forces are keeping a close watch to keep them out of mischief.

'Also, there is talk of Kenyatta being released and the Wakamba are sticking mostly to farming and other less dangerous occupations like wood carving, basket weaving and pottery,' he laughed.

Presently their guest arrived carrying his traditional weapons, greeting his old friend with a warm shake and hug. The other three looked on approvingly; there was certainly no hint of apartheid in bush country.

Mutiso, in line with the standard Bantu race was of medium-short height, stocky build, and with a perennial smile, displaying a set of teeth, perfectly filed, according to tribal custom. Greeting the rest in Swahili, he spoke briefly in his own *Kikamba* tongue to his friend.

After a quick tea sip from their thermoses, they drove off southwards to Kajiado, the small outpost 80 miles from Nairobi. Uncle Bashir knew a shopkeeper at Kajiado where they would stop for lunch, the only stop until they reached their destination on the outskirts of Tsavo.

Johnston and his sidekick stayed with their vehicles, whilst the three others took advantage of the *Gujarati* cuisine. After the meal they rested on their host's veranda for a while.

'Very brave of you to stick it out here in the bush, Rajsinh,' said Bashir to his friend.

'Well, *Rajputs*, the warrior or *Kshatriya* race I belong to, are known for their courage,' replied the host.

Bashir burst out laughing, 'Well there's one more warrior clan for you. Our companions include an African one and I am sure Johnston must have his ancestors tracing their roots back to some Anglo-Saxon warrior tribe, considering his profession!'

'Shekhar what about you, does your family history go back to any Indian fighters?'

The young man smiled. 'No fighting, but I do hail from a community of poets whose job it was, in the old days, to boost the morale of the royalty preceding a battle.'

Uncle concluded, 'that only leaves us Arif. You had better do some investigation, there might be a family link somewhere, although I have my serious doubts,' he said with a wry grin.

Soon after, they departed southwards once more on the dusty route. By evening they reached the outskirts of Tsavo at a Maasai village (*manyatta*) near Samburu and Mtito Andei. The chief came out to greet them with the customary '*Soba.*' Johnston replied likewise and was shown where they could camp for the night. The hunter would contact the game department the following day. The chief told them in detail about the man-eating lions, one of which had been tracked down and killed by the game department only a day or two earlier but the second was still at large.

After setting up camp and dinner the party sat around the camp fire. The hunter discussed his career and regaled them with tales of the jungle, wildlife and his days and nights spent in its midst. The youngsters were eyeing their hosts, the Maasai, for quite a while so their guide first gave them a rough background. 'The Maasai concentrate around the south west of Kenya and more so the north east of (the then) Tanganyika. Being nomads they move around constantly and carry their 'lodgings,' their lightweight huts with them from place to place. Their temporary villages are known as *manyattas*. They use donkeys to carry their other heavy goods. They are identified by their spears and their head dress, made of a lion's mane along with ostrich feathers as you must have observed. When a man kills a lion he is termed a *moran*. Their two favourite drinks are sugarcane mixed with honey and milk mixed with cow's blood. Come with me and I'll show you,' the huntsman said.

A young Maasai approached a cow and from a very short distance released an arrow at the cow's neck, the bleeding cow stood calmly as a sufficient quantity of blood was collected in a tubular vessel and the lad immediately 'patched' up the wound with dry grass and earth. The cow moved away as if nothing had happened while the Maasai downed the 'health' drink at a gulp!

He continued, 'cattle mean everything to the Maasai and considering them God's gift, given the chance they will just walk away with another tribe's cows, usually the Kikuyu. Over the years, they have chased the Kikuyu to the highlands and occupied the savanna for themselves.' The huntsman then turned to his career. 'The association of professional hunters to which I belong, was formed a few years before the war and not just anybody can join. Proficiency in firearms is an obvious must and one has to be a better shot at close range than at a distance considering possibilities of a wounded, charging animal. Safety of the party is paramount.'

'How do you measure a hunter's expertise?' asked Arif.

'Good question, young man,' replied Johnston. 'You ask him the closest distance at which he can shoot comfortably. Were I to be asked, I would say I'm good at about 12-15 metres.'

'Wow,' echoed the boys.

'I sure wouldn't want to be in the proximity of a charging elephant, rhino or lion at that range,' exclaimed Shekhar.

The fire was burning gently, helped by a gentle breeze with occasional prodding by various members of the group as the conversation continued, their faces various shadows, and the darkness contrasting with the burning flames. The sound of crickets in the savannah grasses was the only other sound, with the exception of an occasional distant roar of a lion. Their Maasai hosts in the nearby huts were finishing off for the day.

The teller continued, 'Outstanding knowledge of African wildlife, their habits and of course their habitats is another qualification required, and so is a knowledge of trophy mounting and taxidermy. Often you have to follow the animal, especially if wounded, in the thickest of bush and cover. The idea is not only to finish the hunt but also to end a hurt animal's suffering as soon as possible. This may surprise you boys, but we do respect our wildlife and what I have learned over the years is they are often far wiser than humans.'

Uncle Bashir joined in. 'Well, these boys, the new generation of animal lovers or budding conservationists only came along due to the nature of our safari, getting rid of the man eaters.'

'True, we would rather hunt nasty humans as an alternative, any day,' quipped Arif.

'Well, it may please you to know that hunting with the camera is now on the increase and someday you guys will probably run the likes of me out of business,' laughed the huntsman wryly.

'Mind you, nothing compares to the excitement generated by a hunting safari. One of my biggest moments occurred a few years ago while I was escorting a party up north. We had chased a rhino into the bushes, when it suddenly changed direction and in classic rhino tradition made for us. The animal has eyes to the side of its head and it compensates the poor vision with a strong sense of smell and hearing. We did not have time to shoot and made for tree cover just in time ...

Uncle Bashir apologized and interrupted displaying his knowledge; 'I would say the rhino along with the elephant is one of the most **interesting** as well as *beautiful* among all the African animals, not least due to its lovely horn and a half, weighing over a ton and moving like an army tank. I read somewhere it supersedes the human speed over a 100 metre distance at 28 mph – the human maximising at only 23 mph. No wonder it appears to trot all the way; it uses its **toes** for running!! One could say, *in a bizarre way it is the animal's majestic beauty that causes its downfall via the poachers, as the ignorant fools who kill it, do so for its supposed sex-related/aphrodisiac properties.'*

The hunter continued. 'On the day in question, had it not been for my man here with his accurate arrow expertise I wouldn't be here, recounting this tale,' he finished pointing at his African companion with gratitude.

There was still some time left before they would turn in, so the two youngsters decided to stroll around the camp. 'Don't take too long,' Uncle Bashir called out, 'we've got to rise early for a long day.'

Everyone became aware, the sounds of the wild were getting more and more faint as night approached. Fires around the Maasai camps were still burning, albeit faintly. The shrubland and trees were faint shadows, luckily aided by a full moon bathing what was beneath, in its silvery light. As for above, it was flooded with stars, which sparkled like miniature diamonds, sprawled over a seemingly dark velvety surface, that was the sky.

The softness of the breeze made the ambience complete and as Shekhar drank in the sheer magnificence of untamed Africa, his mate joined him, placing an affectionate palm on his shoulder. 'Nothing to quite compare to it, is there?' he asked.

'I could stand here all night and still not have my fill,' said Shekhar. He suddenly became slightly pensive. 'What do you think will happen in five to ten years' time, if and when Independence comes? You reckon we'll still be around to enjoy all this, which has always been home to us? I mean, most of us and some of our elders too have been born here; I couldn't imagine living anywhere else.'

Arif laughed off his friend's concerns. '*Sikiza, ndugu yangu, sisi ame zaliwa hapo na sisi tuta kufa pia, hapo.* OK?' (listen, my brother, we were born here, and here shall we die ...).

'Anyway, he chuckled, we can discuss your political future tomorrow with the elders, right now we'd better get back and roll down for the night, lest a search party comes looking for us.'

They bedded down in their respective camps. It took a long while to get to sleep, but it finally came.

The gentle sounds of birds chirping as well as human voices speaking softly woke Shekhar. His companions were up he could see, as he peered out of his tent. What greeted him was as beautiful, perhaps more so than what he had observed the night before. The African morn in all its splendour and glory had arrived and he realised there were few things as lovely as seeing it in the wild. The sun was just coming up and the sky was a bright orange, tinged with pink and blue. The savannah grassland was all around them. There were the ubiquitous Acacia trees and other vegetation in the distance including the odd baobab tree doing its impression of a headstand!

'Morning,' greeted the hunter, 'hope you boys had a good night's sleep; there is a stream nearby, wash up and we'll have breakfast.'

They returned presently and with their Maasai hosts having their own brand of breakfast (as above) this group lit a fire, eggs and beans sizzling, while Kenya-grown coffee was being brewed alongside. Johnston went off to see the local Game Warden about the lion, while the others stayed at camp.

Man-eating lions were quite common at the turn of century when during the construction of the Kenya-Uganda railway many Indians as well as a few white colonials lost their lives. But the recent man-eaters were isolated cases as their guide explained.

He returned after a couple of hours. 'Well,' he said, 'I've got all the background. The surviving one at large is a male lion probably wounded. As you might or might not know, these fellows only kill humans due to necessity – a last resort, when they are unable to chase animal prey due to old age, a wound in a fight or an escaped shoot. This one is particularly wily and the (game) department has, try as they might, been unable to get him. He seems to hang out in the thickest parts of the growth and waits for his chance with vulnerable humans.'

The hunters started off and as agreed Uncle Bashir would follow in his vehicle at a considerable, visible distance. The main hunting party also took with them a young Maasai for pointing out recent areas where unfortunate victims had been attacked. The last one was a youth grazing his cattle and probably strayed out of the safety zone. They covered quite a vast area and were slowly losing heart.

'The last thing I want is the night to overtake us and stretch this to tomorrow,' said Johnston. He then conferred with his companions and seemed to have made some sort of final strategy.

Transferring his companion, the Kikamba, to the second vehicle, he approached the bush, albeit with caution with the Maasai armed with his conventional spear, more for moral support than anything else. This thick undergrowth was only one of two covering a large area and having scouted the other there was a good chance that they would find their quarry here.

Something moved among the bushes, a shot was fired and everyone heard the Lion roar and move out into the open at the edge. He rushed towards Johnston, who stood his ground, took aim and emptied two consecutive bullets from his .450 light bore rifle. Simultaneously, with the second rifle shot, an arrow left the bow of the trusted Kikamba; this was the insurance. If the bullet missed, the arrow would do the job. With three armaments released one after the other the beast did not have a chance.

A moment earlier all those present saw the proud king of the jungle almost dive onto his would-be assailant and the next, the entire poundage thump onto the ground, lifeless. A huge mass of dry earth was displaced, rising as a miniature cloud where the animal fell, and save the sound of a large flock of birds which took off from a tree, disturbed by the gun shots, everything fell completely silent for the next few moments ...

The teenagers in the second vehicle had seen their first and they hoped, last, hunt.

The first sound was that of the jubilant Maasai youth who had accompanied them, jumping, dancing and whooping away. He would be the one conveying these good tidings to his village folk and there would no doubt be celebrations with the hunters hailed as heroes.

Uncle Bashir asked only half-jokingly, 'Is it safe to come out now?' The proud marksman raised his hand in assent, 'Well that was some shooting and by both of you.' He turned and smiled at the African.

'Under other circumstances the dead animal would have been carried back to the village inversely on a pole, for all to see, here, though it'll be sufficient to take a small part of the lion's anatomy as proof of our successful expedition,' said the man of the moment as they made their way back to the campsite.

That evening, the entourage of five were guests at the village. Large fires, traditional dancing and dinner, courtesy of the village chief were in order. The inhabitants could rest easy now and cattle grazing and other activities involving the more vulnerable members – women and children – could continue without fear.

The Maasai killed a large buck and the animal was roasted on a spit. When dance followed, it was still dusk and darkness had not yet arrived. There was a grin on Shekhar's face as they were viewing the dance, since, as the male dancers jumped about one could see parts of their anatomy which would normally be unexposed. This was rather like a Scotsman and his kilt and as Arif looked at his friend, Shekhar explained, 'I know we're all men here, but I just remembered a slightly different situation. Some guests had visited our family from the sub-continent, ladies included, and whilst on safari, they happened to visit a Maasai dance. You can imagine the embarrassment on the faces of the ladies, the poor things didn't know where to look!'

They all had a good laugh. Suddenly Arif, remembering the day's hunt asked, 'Sir, have you ever been frightened during any of your hunts?'

'Sure, many a time. In fact, there is a saying in these parts that a hunter pursuing a lion, is frightened not once, but thrice. First when he sees the animal's tracks, second when he hears the lion's roar and finally when he comes face to face with his quarry and looks it in the eye. Nothing to be ashamed of, we all hunters go through it.'

They had had a long day and were looking forward to the main part of their safari the next day and hence they turned in early.

Early next morning after a quick breakfast they made

for the eastern part of Tsavo Royal National Park – as it was then known – and which also houses the Mzima Springs.

Their guide explained, 'the best time to view the wild-life is the first three hours of daylight, which arrives invariably at around 6 a.m. throughout the year so we'll have to be up with the lark.'

Since there was no shortage of fauna the youths made full use of their binoculars and cameras. Also, there was no dearth of natural beauty abounding in this, the eastern and more picturesque half of the park as com-pared to the western part which is more rugged with mountain ranges.

They stopped briefly for some snacks after an hour's drive and just as they re-started their vehicles, some-thing huge appeared in their way. A large bull elephant devouring any and all vegetation in his path decided to stop in front of them. With tall savannah grasses on both sides and this giant in between there was nothing else to do but wait. They all sat together in one vehicle. Suddenly from the rear of the Land Rover came soft musical notes; they all looked to the rear. It was Mutiso, who had broken into song, *Twende sa-fa-riiii* (crescen-do), *twende safari,* (flat) *amuli ya naani? Amuli ya Jomo Kenyatta amuli ya Kenya* ... (let's go on safari in the name of Jomo Kenyatta ...)

Twende Nai-ku-ruuuu (Nakuru), (again high) *twende naikuru* (flat), *amuli ya naani?* ...

'So, you are a singer as well, Mutiso,' said the boys. Their guide laughed, 'My friend goes into melody every time we are in such a fix. Helps us all relieve a bit of our boredom,' he said with a wink. 'Meanwhile until his lordship in front of us decides to move, we'll have a drink or two.' So saying the hunter opened up a can of Tusker(!) (Tusker is a popular Kenyan beer as well as a nickname for the African elephant.)

While they waited for the 'lord of the jungle' to move, the two elders discussed more serious issues pertaining to wildlife. 'As you must know, Bashir, Kenya only began "feeling" for *conservation* of wild life in place of the negative concept of mere *preservation*, after the second war. By that time not only the hunting "sportsmen" from all over the world who killed animals in thousands, but the two wars, rising population, native-owned cattle and closer settlement all contributed to the colossal decline in fauna. People like Lord Delamere made futile suggestions which were only implemented years later when the first national parks were created and not without assistance from other animal lovers. Still, even as we speak, there is serious decline in rhino and lion population; elephants were also on the list but have in recent years increased, however they are being compressed into smaller areas which then brings about conflict with humans! However, steps are being taken albeit slowly, whereby the animals like the rhino are being transferred to reserves where they will have sufficient grazing areas. Here in Tsavo itself, the biggest stronghold, nearly half of the rhino population has perished due to malnutrition, so I hope action is taken soon. Similarly, lions and lion cubs especially in the Mara region are under threat from humans and predators respectively, man-eaters being a separate issue altogether.'

The youngsters had been listening intently and Shekhar at last joined in: 'Mr Johnston, talking of conservation, the real hero of the hour, and one I am sure we would all be honoured to meet would be Mervyn Cowie, who I have read, has worked tirelessly, more than anyone, for the protection of East African wildlife and helped create all the wonderful reserves and national parks.'

'I can't disagree with you there,' said the seeker. 'There are a number of wonderful incidents to show how he managed all that. When he returned from further studies in the U.K. in 1932 he began his campaign, which of course, was ignored. So, he played a ruse whereby he advocated the killing of all wildlife in Kenya apparently in order to benefit agriculture. The public outcry did the trick and ultimately the first animal reserve, the Nairobi National Park was created in 1946, followed by others including the Tree Tops in 1952 and ones in Uganda and Tanganyika.'

Skekhar added, 'Another incident similar to the hunter turned conservationist Jim Corbett's experience (mentioned later) took place when Cowie riding through the Nairobi National Park reserve fell off his motorbike. He lay there bleeding as a lioness passing by watched him. The smell of petrol from the motorbike apparently was stronger than the smell of blood and the animal after observing the human for a while, just walked away harmlessly. The young Mervyn realised then, that man and animal could co-exist without difficulty if only man could overcome his desire to keep killing animals for "sport" as well as give them places to thrive.' Conversation on conservation came to an end finally as the elephant moved away and the journey continued.

Various animals like the rhino, cheetah, baboons and the giraffe were seen. Their guide gave interesting details of each species. 'The elephant, as you boys might know are one close animal to humans, in the way they move in family-fashion, communicate via tummy rumbles and the way they mourn their dead. They apparently have very sharp memories remembering previously visited sites long before. We have already discussed the rhinoceros. Then there is the giraffe; their huge eyelashes would make any glamorous female envious, not to speak of their sharp eyesight especially at their height! They have especially long tongues which they use often at angles to obtain one of their favourite foods, the leaves of the acacia trees! There are about eight different species in Africa but you would have to examine their body patterns very closely to realise the variation. They are often hunted by the lion but whereas the lion, faster at 50mph, moves in short bursts, the giraffe at 30mph can move steadily for long periods. Also, when confronted their long-legged kicks are lethal to the predator! The cheetah as you might know is the fastest land animal reaching a top speed of 70mph in a mere six to seven seconds. The baboon monkeys funny though they are in appearance with their unique 'rear view,' seize every opportunity to steal food or whatever is available from humans!

They saw a warthog running from a predator and were delighted to see that upon reaching its underground burrow it ingeniously turned backwards and stopped the predator in its tracks as it was ready to attack it with its sharp warts!

'Most of the animals seem to be oblivious to our presence,' remarked Shekhar. 'This in spite of poaching* by locals and foreign guys who hire them for the ivory, the rhino horn as aphrodisiacs of all things – and other trophies. The rangers do their best, but poisoned arrows, pits or snares do their dirty work nevertheless.'

'Compared to these chaps us hunters are not such a bad lot, are we?' half-smirked Johnston.

In addition to the wild animals they had the opportunity to be amazed by the flora as well. The short October rains had been delayed and after the relentless heat of the dry season, within a matter of days the entire landscape was turned into an Eden, ornamented with lush green grass, shrubs and creepers and an excellent display of flower of every imaginable colour.

* Today 30,000 African elephants are killed annually – one every fifteen minutes – by poachers. Europe, Britain and the Far East are all involved in this trade one way or the other. As for the rhinoceros, their killing goes on at the rate of one every eight hours, the poaching having increased nine-fold in the last five years!

They finally reached the springs located at around 25 miles from Mtito Andei just as it was getting hot and the sun overhead. They opened their cans of food and drink plus Indian savouries that came in handy.

The hunter's commentary had rattled on non-stop. 'I can well understand now how your tours are booked months in advance,' commented Uncle Bashir, 'you never let a dull moment creep in.'

Once again, the party was both delighted as well as astounded by what they saw. Set in a parched valley scattered with lava ash boulders an innumerable amount of crystal clear water emerged with suddenness and created indescribably lovely pools which became the water home of the hippo, crocodile and a colourful variety of fish. They relaxed under the lush trees that abounded occasionally feeding the fish but keeping well clear of the hippos and crocodiles.

The final 'commentary of the safari' was relayed, 'The hippo are the biggest members in sustaining a food chain, browsing on the savannah grass at night and fertilising the spring waters with dung during the day. This in turn enables the various fruit trees to thrive: dates, raffia palms and figs obtain nutrients via their roots which submerge into the water and feed vervet monkeys and cormorant and other birds as well as fish who finally feed on the various invertebrates present in the water who thrive on hippo dung!! And finally, one more for your diaries, lads, the hippos are the biggest human killers in Africa taking more than a hundred victims each year!

The hunter finally observed with a hint of mirth the drained expressions on his 'nature study' students and concluded 'enough for now lads. Here endeth the lesson!'

The evening shadows arrived and as they packed their gear and bade their farewell to Mzima, they observed one more beautiful display of Africa's infinite beauty. Of the several shades and colours they had observed and enjoyed during the day light hours, only two were visible to wish them on their way. The velvety black shadows displayed by the landscape as well as the flora contrasting perfectly with the bright, bold orange sky and sun amidst the last hints of fading daylight ...

They returned by late evening for what was going to be their last camp night. Some of the Maasai elders came and sat by the camp fire and thanked Johnston and his mate for their services as had the game department when the hunter had visited them the previous day.

Finally, before turning in, Shekhar asked 'Bwana, you must have known quite a few hunters during your time, let's hear about the best among them.'

'You mean, besides myself?' laughed Johnston. 'Well, there were some before my time, whom I obviously never met, like W.D.M. Bell aka Karamoja Bell, who hunted with a light bore-275 rifle considered probably the most accurate shooter of elephants. Then there is J.A. Hunter who has just completed the Hunter's Lodge Hotel at Makindu this year and, lastly, I had the pleasure of meeting Jim Corbett twice just before his death a few years ago.'

'Corbett was a hunter turned conservationist, wasn't he? He spent years in India hunting tigers, which he recounted in his books before moving to Kenya after Indian Independence,' Uncle Bashir joined in.

'What most people probably do not know, as described in his story, *The last hunt*, is how he gave up hunting in favour of conservation,' said Shekhar. 'I read he had shot and wounded a tiger during one of his hunts whilst in India and as he followed to finish him off, he saw the animal lying helpless in some grassland. What he wrote next is unbelievable but those were his own words. The tiger which was minutes from death, was struggling with its paws and appeared to have tears in its eyes. Corbett wrote that he threw away his rifle that instant and never hunted again.'

The rest of them were silent for a moment, but Johnston commented, 'Well, no offence to the grand old man but I have yet to see this sort of miracle and until I do, my rifle will remain loaded.'

He continued, 'As for J.A., he is one of the biggest and best among living ones and he also has authored several books. At the Makueni hunting ground location he killed nearly 1,000 rhinos in just two months just after the war, at the government's request as the Wakambas were to be re-settled there,' he pointed to his friend.

'How disgusting,' the boys echoed.

'Well he regretted it as much, particularly as the land proved to be useless for settlement anyway, so you can blame Mutiso and his people for being the cause of the carnage,' the hunter said with half a sneer.

The fire was about to extinguish and the sounds of the wild had also died down, so with a final yawn, the huntsman gave his final instructions, 'Well, gentlemen, on that note we shall turn in for the night and make tracks towards Nairobi, come morning.'

The return journey, like all return journeys seemed comparatively short. They stopped at Makindu, an inevitable stop for Indians at the Sikh Temple where round the clock *Langar* (food blessed before its offered to guests) is served. As Johnston was to pay a visit to the Hunters' Lodge, Uncle Bashir jokingly invited their African helper *'Wachana na huyu Mzungu naenda kwa jamaa zake, sisi tuta tumia dengu na chapatti kwa maskiti wa kalasinga* (with a hint of sarcasm: Let this white man visit his kinsfolk, whilst we visit the Sikh Temple for chapatis and lentils).

They then talked about the Temple. It was built as far back as 1926 during the construction of the Kenya-Uganda railway although a makeshift one had been around since the completion of the railway in 1902. The shrine was built as a homage to the first guru of the

Sikhs, Guru Nanak.

After lunch, they met their guide at an agreed place in town and made their way to the final stop before Nairobi. The boys and their elder had a surprise in store as they all made to a boys' school in Marangu near Machakos where Mutiso stayed. The African had his son studying there and it transpired that Johnston too had someone of his studying there. After a bit of questioning the guests found that their huntsman was sponsoring an African boy at the school. All three were filled with admiration.

They said their goodbyes to the native, who would wait for his friend's communication a month later for their next expedition. 'This one concerns rampaging elephants,' said their man. 'In some parts of the country it is man versus beast. This largest mammal on earth consumes tons of vegetation daily and now a choice has to be made.'

It was late evening by the time they arrived home in Parklands, Nairobi. Their guide wanted to leave but not before a sundowner arranged by the family and a light supper. As it turned dark, the man said his farewell. 'I'm meeting someone at the Norfolk (hotel) and will stay there the night.'

As they parted, he smiled at the boys, 'Well, *vijana* (youngsters) I hope you have had a good time. Maybe someday we'll all go for a photo safari, once your "lobbyists" succeed in banning hunting.'

'Unlikely, for a while at least,' said his friend Bashir.

As the Land Rover moved off the three looked on and waved.

The elder said, 'Well, boys there goes probably one of the last of a dying species – the human kind, I mean.'

The boys stood there for a while, silently. At last Arif spoke on behalf of both. 'A hunter who cares for animals, a colonial who befriends and adopts natives! Wouldn't have believed it in a hundred years.'

'Neither will our mates at school, until we show them the photographs,' said his friend as they made their way to the veranda.

They would not forget the better part of the previous week for a long time to come. As Shekhar took an impulsive glance behind, all he could see was the African night and the darkness, with the guard dogs now unchained.

He could not prevent his mind racing back a 100 miles plus, down the Nairobi Mombasa high road. The beauty, the rawness, that they had experienced and often in the dark was, in a sense, similar to the darkness that engulfed them now, and yet ... undoubtedly ... so very, very different!!

Chapter 20

G.C.E.: The Exam Monster·:
A whole lot of 'swotting' and a hint of poetry for relief!

Subsequent to their Jungle Safari, Shekhar and Arif spent a few more days together in Nairobi before returning to their coastal abode to finish the rest of their vacation.

The final year would arrive soon and the boys were supposed to start preparations for their G.C.E. Examinations early in the year. Of course, however like most, illustrious(!) students it was the last couple of months when real action took place. The year had been spent more on sports and visits to the Mombasa Girls' School, but now the G.C.E. Exams were beckoning.

The gang of five, as in everything else, burnt midnight oil together. The hot, balmy nights ensured they kept awake for much of the time, aided by cups of coffee as well as splashing soda water to their eyes which apparently helps in keeping awake!

They studied and slept in rotation at each friend's house. This went on for the whole of the last month and towards the end there was hardly any sleep. When they kicked each other awake in the early hours of the morn, they could invariably hear the musically minded Indrajeet singing away in the shower.

Their initial irritation brought shouts of, 'Would somebody ask Mr Mohammed Rafi (the singer icon of the

* this is how students often referred to the Exam.

times) to shut up while we grab forty winks for the remaining few minutes.' However, the choice of song with its touch of ironic humour brought much needed cheer at the time, one of which was: *Hum dard ke maaron ka itna hi fasana hai!* (you get the pun, see below) and better still, *Parwar digare aalam tera hi hai sahara, tere siva jahan mein koi nahin hamara!*

(Rough translation):

1) This is our tale of woe and all that we miserable sods are fit for (In the actual film-song situation the character is an alcoholic; thus his tale of woe relates to his alcoholic state and not really the kind of misery or plight the students were undergoing!)

2) *Parwar digare aalam ...* is a prayer and call to the Almighty, and translated simply means 'O great Almighty, thou art the only hope, no one but thee in the entire universe can we call our own' (in these times of distress!).

Well, the Almighty does help those who help themselves, and the relentless efforts of the group at last bore fruit when the exam papers and ultimately the results too, were to their liking, for the most part anyway.

On exam days, they did their 'swotting' right up to the last minutes and *Mummyji,* being the mother of whichever mate's residence they were at, 'stuffed' *parathas* into their mouths along with helpings of yoghurt, the latter of which according to Indian custom brings good luck to the task at hand.

Most papers were sailed through with relative ease, however geography was one paper where some students were tempted to leave the hall half way through.

There was a famous little tale about exam papers and a verse relating thereto, going around during those days which went something like this:

A certain student, not having prepared for his exams,

wrote the following lines on his otherwise blank answer paper, *Hazaron ki quismat tere PAAS hai, agar PASS kar de to kya baat hai?* (The fate of thousands rests in your hands, what would be the harm if you gave a pass-mark?)

The examiner, one step ahead, wrote the reply: *Kitabon ki chaabi tere PAAS thi, agar YAAD kar leta to kya baat thi?* (The 'key' to the study/exam was in your hands, what would have been the HARM if you had cared to use it?)

Fortunately, our lads did not have to resort to such tomfoolery and the final results were favourable to most in the group.

'Till we meet again' ...

After four years of lessons and sport and other 'activities' it was time to say goodbye to old mates and teachers, some gladly, others with sadness. Further studies, into the professions, family businesses and, yes, some would even become teachers themselves.

Shekhar and cousin Nilesh decided to go for further studies to India. As they would ultimately join the family law firm they would pursue a Law Degree (along with a basic Arts graduation as was the requirement).

It would be a while before the cousins returned to their beloved country, except for holidays and they would find it a changed Kenya, with the arrival of *Uhuru* (Independence) in 1963 and to some extent, its repercussions ...

Chapter 21

Departure for further studies (law degree) ... and return ...

After their G.C.E. exams Shekhar and Nilesh had a meeting with the family, particularly the Dads. It was pretty much decided by all that the two eldest siblings would pursue a law degree (the normal practice/requirement on the sub-continent is to do basic graduation in the arts and then follow it up with a law degree) and upon completion, return and join the family firm, learn the ropes and gradually take over from their elders.

Thus, the decade of the '60s saw the two young men depart for the Indian sub-continent. A few of their mates joined them, some to read accountancy, others medicine and yet some who were in a hurry, a simple commerce or arts degree. At one stage, the Vakils had considered the United Kingdom, but financial and more than a couple of other factors prevented this alternative.

Uhuru!

Subsequent to the end of the Mau Mau emergency and fight for independence, the movement leader Jomo Kenyatta was imprisoned and then released at the end of the decade. Independence – Uhuru – was at last on the cards. Other African countries were also in a state of political revolt. In 1960, Belgian Congo got independence from its colonial masters (followed by mayhem and murder of their leader the following year with many Congolese taking refuge in Kenya, but that is another story ...). Neighbouring Uganda and Tanganyika (and then with Zanzibar island, becoming Tanzania) were granted independence in subsequent years. Kenya was the last in line, becoming independent in 1963 and a republic the following year.

Shekhar and his cousin kept a close, albeit limited watch via telephone calls home, media coverage and more via post, considering the limited communication of those times, of the unfolding of the political events. They visited Kenya every one or two years and finally the day came when it was time for them to return to their beloved country.

Homeward bound ...

Visiting India – and return – in those days was invariably by sea unless you were able to afford air travel and the cousins like their friends, made their way from Bombay via steamship *SS Karanja* which they and others had boarded several times before in recent years.

Travel by boat was a holiday within a holiday. Here students from various parts of the African continent travelled together every year or two becoming not only co-travellers, but close buddies. They enjoyed the freshness of the sea breeze as well as the waves which was most invigorating. Daytime deck games, music sessions (the elders sang devotional songs), night time social activities, super meals and (soft) drinks thrice a day (unless you were, unfortunately in the 'sea sick' category! Family entertainment (bingo ...) provided by the captain and his team and movies every other day. Small wonder then, everyone seemed sad when the voyage ended.

On the way, one stoppage in the Indian Ocean was at the lovely islands of Seychelles which were arrived at five days after setting sail. Anchoring in the islands' harbour those who wished to visit, disembarked onto small boats to spend a few hours and get a taste of things to come.

The beautiful islands boasted lovely vegetation including palm trees and other, flowering plants. Tortoises are a common sight and rides are available – by the minute/s – considering their speed! as are toys made from their (patterned) shells. Other curios and artefacts include the famous conch shells as well as drinking vessels made from coconut shells, pearl necklaces and stones in various colours. Presently one heard the ship's siren, beckoning the passengers. The boys filled their 'boots' with curios for the family members in addition to the load of presents they had purchased on the sub-continent.

After seven days of sail the ship arrived at the Kilindini harbour of Mombasa. Family members, with delight on their faces all, were waiting to receive the various passengers. Radha and Reshma rushed to their *Motabhai*, Shekhar and the more sober Nilesh with affectionate hugs. The ladies prepared sweets on this auspicious day. The cousins spent the evening and next day regaling their days on the sub-continent.

Learning the ropes at the office

Kakaji took charge and began training the young men as he was getting on in years and wished to take things easy. The family firm had expanded and after a while a family meeting was called, including the domestic help as well as Esmail, the chauffeur.

After some small talk, Dad came to the point. 'Now

that Shekhar and Nilesh have come back we are ready to take the big step that *Motabhai* and myself have been planning for some time. We have decided to move to Nairobi. Many of our clients are based there and besides avoiding frequent travelling, there would be several other advantages. Mombasa, although we shall miss it, is just not big enough for us.' He waited for the reaction from family members. The ladies had already been informed.

The twins Radha and Reshma now in their teens were delighted and made no secret of it, as they had a number of friends upcountry as well as a favourite or two among their cousins. The elder cousins including sister Geeta were all for the move as well. Arif, Shekhar's close friend had shifted to Nairobi some time back.

Ali expressed his feelings, 'Bwana, I have had enough of this house work and wish to go into the catering business, which has, as you all know, been my real passion all along.' Everyone looked glum. Ali had always been a member of the family and life without him was unimaginable.

Dad thought for a while and both brothers came up with a possible solution almost simultaneously. 'Why don't we contact Shamji, the hotelier in Nairobi. He has a large outfit and I'm sure he would be glad to have you on his team, Ali. I think I speak on behalf of everybody when I say we'd hate to have you out of our sights and that too at a distance of 300 miles!'

Everyone seemed relieved for the present, at least.

Esmail the driver was getting on in years so he would remain behind. Osman would be the main domestic; he had somebody in mind who would do the double duties of gardening plus limited house work. Within a couple of days, the hotel job for Ali was confirmed; he would always be available in emergencies and on special occasions.

Thus, the Vakils left the coastal paradise and with a

heavy heart, since the place had been home to them for a good part of two decades ...

It was the mid-60s now when the family arrived at their new abode. The menfolk had made a couple of trips and with the help of a client, selected a house between Parklands and Westlands, which were the Asian property stronghold. Large lounge, kitchen, diner, five spacious bedrooms, two bathrooms and a magnificent landscaped garden plus carport. They would miss the sea but the elder members seemed to be relieved with the cooler highland temperatures in preference to the coast's sticky heat.

The new practice took off just as they had hoped, what with the large clientele they had already established over the years and prominent new ones. This, with the arrival of the young blood as well as new staff, including a young African graduate who wanted to train before starting off on his own. Gradually the two elders began to take things easy and that included *Kakiji* who concentrated more on giving private tuition to high school students.

Moving upcountry to the capital had leisure advantages too. Proximity to game reserves as well as the Rift Valley, highlands and other towns meant that Shekhar with his love for nature often utilised weekends with friends in exploring these sights.

A special event that the friend circle would follow keenly would be the East African Safari which had Nairobi as a starting point for Kenya.

The 1965 safari was going to be special, with, among other things a new title, 'The East African safari rally' ...

Chapter 22

Safari ...!

It was Easter holiday time. Four days of rest and relaxation from the routine and for the enthusiastic public of which there was no dearth, the Safari Rally which would be spread over the entire Easter period. The long rains of April would make it even more gruelling and test the contestants' expertise to the limit. Small wonder that it was without dispute termed the number one long distance car race in the world.

The term *safari* has been applied to various subjects as in hunting safaris, jungle safaris and the like. Interestingly the standard attire too, for some of the hotter tropics are termed safari suits! Derived apparently from the Hindi/Urdu *safar* meaning journey, the rally was incepted as the Coronation Safari in 1953 upon Queen Elizabeth's accession to the throne. It became the East African Safari in 1960 and finally the (Kenya) Rally in the 1970s. For the ordinary public it became a 'day or days out' as well.

Meghji Shah was a businessman, a friend as well as a client of the firm, and a huge fan of the Rally. *Kakaji* and the businessman often played bridge at the Gymkhana. M.S. as he was fondly known among friends, was one more Vakil acquaintance who lived life to the full. His huge and stylish home was a venue for parties as well as musical functions. Whenever an artiste arrived from the Indian sub-continent you could be sure of a musical evening at his place. Come Easter and Shek-har's family would be invited to join the former and friends for a day out, and a picnic, usually on Good Friday and subsequent to the send-off to the contestants from City Hall in Nairobi on Thursday evening.

His phone communications to friends began a week prior to the event and with fervour. 'Be at mine on time on Thursday, it's going to be a big one this year' – For M.S., every year's safari was invariably going to be 'a big one'!! Crates of Tusker beer and Coca Cola, and cartons of samosas, bhajias and other goodies would be packed full in his (additional) van and off they would go on Good Friday morning at a chosen spot en route the rally.

The 1965 rally created much excitement for the rally enthusiasts, for this year the race had been given its new title of the East African Safari Rally. The origins of the rally went back as far as 1950 when the then chair-man of the Automobile Association of East Africa, Eric Cecil, came up with the idea of a long-distance safari (quote: 'I can imagine nothing more boring than driving/racing round and round the same piece of racing track') and along with his cousins travelled from Nairo-bi to Cape Town, South Africa and back with record timing.

Inspired by the foregoing it was decided to hold a rally between the three East African territories over the Easter holiday period, which came to be known as the Coronation Safari. In time it became an unrivalled world rally drawing car manufacturing teams from the USA (Detroit) to Japan, covering a huge distance with starting points in all the three East African territories. Vic Preston and D.P. Marwaha were the class winners in the first year (1953) and overall winners in 1954, and 1955. Motor sport was always very popular in East Africa with racing tracks at Nakuru, the agricultural capital and other venues. The rally became an advert for the various car manufacturing companies and the general public loved it and thronged at small centres throughout the length and breadth of the three countries, sometimes keeping vigil all night, serving food and drink for drivers who required it. It was the year's biggest and best sporting event. Lady drivers also participated. Best cars for safari conditions turned out to be Germany's VW Beetle and Mercedes and the French, Peugeot the Ford Zephyr and Swedish Volvo.

Shekhar and a couple of friends who always took a keen interest in the rally made their way to City Hall, the starting point. Dilip, who had arrived from Mombasa commented, 'Joginder and Jaswant, the Singh brothers are hot favourites this year. Since 1960 they've always finished in the race, though never won outright, having, in 1963, finished fourth.'

In the event, amidst much cheering from the public, their name came out of the drum ballot first. Thus, they were car number one; previously only once had number one been the winner.

'Looks like it's going to be a record send off this year,' Shekhar observed.

All enthusiasts managed to reach City Hall by 6 p.m. on Thursday and stayed on until dark when the first 30 cars rolled off the ramp and this despite a record crowd of approximately 30,000 strong and fully geared up. The police had their work cut out in containing them. The remainder would follow on television which had arrived in 1962 to this country. Although transmitted in black and white, the public was glued to it over Easter, throwing the likes of *Bonanza* and *Top Cat* to one side.

Due to the long rains in April, and particularly this year, it was going to be a nastily wet and muddy event. As per usual practice, M.S. and his entourage of three cars left for Athi River which is 15-20 miles south of

Nairobi towards Mombasa. They left just before noon on Good Friday and arrived around lunchtime. En route they noticed, as during all rallies, growing crowds of African children and adults all enthusiastic and waving away.

Shekhar jokingly remarked, whilst driving his recently acquired Toyota, to the accompanying Dilip, 'But for the absence of a rally number and accessories on our cars, they might as well be cheering for us!'

They camped by the popular picnic spot at the Athi River with the river flowing nearby.

After their lunch, courtesy Mr Shah, who had gone just that bit overboard with his menu this time in place of his usual and simple 'Beer and Samosa' package. His community friend and a fellow Lion (Club) inquired: 'What's up, M.S. chicken and biryani in place of the usual?'

Replied Meghjibhai: 'Well, J.K., ask me that question on Easter Monday, when Joginder and Jaswant fly in ahead of all the others,' he forecasted proudly, making a flying gesture with his palm.

Everyone present wished his prediction came true. A couple of his friends, who always seized such opportunities, wagered small bets in favour of past winners who were also hot favourites this year.

'No chance,' challenged the Mistry brothers who loved betting.

'Mia moja hapo (one hundred here) says it will be the Swedish Erik Carlson and brother-in-law Stirling Moss this year as well.'

After lunch, the group split into two, some playing cards and others having a siesta. On their return journey, the crowds had increased considerably. They passed the popular residential locality of Nairobi South C and Nairobi West and prior to that the Belle Vue drive-in cinema, which mostly showed Indian films. One thing was certain. The earlier 7 p.m. show, would definitely be a dead loss from the look of things!!

Enthusiasts kept track via TV and Radio for the next two days and waited with baited breath for the last stretch.

On Easter Monday, the final day, the Shah group was up early. They headed all the way to Machakos – 35 miles down Mombasa onwards, the public/fans more or less knew who the champion *wa Myaka* (of the year) 1965 was going to be.

'I hear the Singh brothers have taken a gigantic amount of pounding in their Volvo PV-544 during their 3,000-mile ordeal plus more than ten punctures en route,' said one member to the group.

When they hit the outskirts of the capital, jubilations began ... Punjabis performing their *Bhangra* and the local African cheering, *'kara (kala) singha ame ingia, ame shinda!'* (the Singh/s have arrived, have won!)

The victors had beaten the runners-up, the Jaffray/Bathhurst team in their Peugeot 404 by a cool and clear 100 minutes finally reaching City Hall with a colossal public uproar to make their victory complete. The only lady finishers were Lucette Pointer and Francoise in their Peugeot.

Needless to say, the celebrations continued long into the night, the public disregarding that next day would be a working day – except for those on leave or school holidays. The Sikh brothers lived on Blenheim Road, Parklands, which was opposite the Nairobi Museum and Meghjibhai who knew people in the Automobile Association took his entourage to meet and congratulate the flying Sikh or *Simba wa Kenya* (Lion of Kenya) as Joginder would henceforth be known. He went on to win the rally in future years as well.

The victory was of special significance due to having

been won by the first locals or Kenyans as well as the first all Indian team.

It was nearly midnight when Shekhar and mates made their way home, which was only a few miles down the Road, doing a detailed 'post mortem' of the event on the way ...

Chapter 23

Mike: *Mwafrica Baniyani!* (the African *Bania)*

The Vakils, over the next couple of years, expanded the firm, with a cosmopolitan client list comprising amongst others Asian businessmen, professionals, a couple of English farmers and upcoming African members of the public some of whom had just started out in small business

One such small businessman was a middle-aged Kikuyu gentleman, Michael Kimathi for whom the firm handled a small case.

A few weeks later he walked into the firm's offices, looking rather apprehensive. Earlier he had dealt with *Uncleji* who found him as an honest sort. Today, however, he seemed to have something special on his mind. He had started a small business and the bank would lend him only a certain amount without any real security. He wanted a loan for a thousand shillings, a fair amount at the time.

Kakaji was out of the office, so it was Shekhar who took him into his cabin.

'Yes, *Bwana Mkuba* (big boss), what can I do for you?' asked the young lawyer who had begun to charm his way into the hearts and minds of his various clients over the months and years.

At first Mike as he was known to all, hesitated but then opened up, and stated his requirement.

Shekhar asked a few questions and the satisfactory response plus his previous knowledge of the customer via *Kakaji* enabled him to make up his mind. True to his easy going and kind nature part inherited from his uncle, he agreed to give him a personal or rather private loan as it had nothing to do with the firm:

'*Asante saana* (thank you very much), young Mr Vakil. This is going to give my business a real cash injection,' laughed Mike, displaying his toothy grin at the same time. 'You know, *sisi kyuk*· (we Kikuyus) are the *banyanis* among the Kenyan tribes,' he proudly asserted his heritage, 'and b*iashara* (business) is in our blood. As is well known, we Kikuyu are the prominent Kenyan tribe, into farming and other businesses and the fertile highlands mostly belong to us,' he further proclaimed.

His repayments were regular initially, but then towards the end dwindled off and the Vakils did not see him for a couple of years. Then, one day he strolled into the offices unexpectedly.

Dressed smart in an expensive looking pin-stripe, most likely purchased from one of the Government Road Indian Draperies, he caused all in the office to stand awestruck! Laughing heartily in his deep voice he embraced his benefactor, his eyes brimming with emotion along with an apology for the delay in the final payments. He announced with a touch of classic Swahili-English, 'Yes it's me my dear friends, the very one. Michael Jameson Kimathi.'

He continued, 'I have purchased a farm at Limuru in the highlands from a *mzungu*, a smaller one at Kiambu and also acquired some small properties in the capital's township at *Kariokor* and *Pangani* which I have rented out. I have been *so very* busy and you must forgive me for the delay.' Shekhar as well as his elders could see that the man had lost none of his humility and gentle charm despite his financial rise as was evident from his smart suiting and other attire.

---

* as they sometimes refer to themselves.

Shekhar smiled, 'I had written off the outstanding amount, but if you insist(!) I'll accept the balance; do not worry about the interest, we're all delighted with your progress.' The seniors offered tea to the unexpected visitor and before parting, Mike said, 'My dear friends, please accept my invitation to come and "eat goat" at my farm residence at Kiambu next Sunday if you are free.'

The invitation was accepted, but not without reservations. Dad expressed this with a grin, 'How on earth are we going to persuade our strict vegetarian womenfolk to come and "eat goat" with us? Not that we are too keen either, despite our occasional indulgence in non- vegetarian cuisine!' Using all their inherent tact, the menfolk managed to persuade the ladies, who conveniently reminded them, 'It's the religious month anyway, so we shall be keeping a fruit fast.'

'Well that is a stroke of luck, otherwise we're in a real fix, not wanting to offend our host at any cost,' Dad sighed with relief.

On Sunday, the family, in their six-seater, the four elders accompanied by Shekhar and sister Geeta departed by mid-morning. The route to Kiambu was green, at times raw and earthy at others, cultivated and orderly, an endless carpet of coffee plants adorning the road both left and right.

'This is real, rural Kenya,' said Geeta, as they entered the township, 'which back in Nairobi we hardly come across.'

'Well, certainly not our lot,' added Shekhar.

They saw African bars, playing local music in Swahili and dialect vocals to the strums of steel guitars and gentle African drums beats. The radio played famous adverts:

'*Sigara yangu, Sigara Yako,* Crown Bird, (cigarette mine, cigarette yours, *Crown Bird*)

Shillingi Moja na peni tatu, Crown Bird' ... (one shilling and three pence, *Crown Bird*)

Television had arrived a few years earlier and local Swahili sitcoms such as *Jamaa ya Mzee Pembe* (the family of Mister/Boss Pembe) were on display in public places. Locals ate *boflo* (bread dunked in tea) and *chai*. Children, dogs and chicken played in sandy compounds of a few stone houses, but these were overshadowed by huts with thatched roofs and other small stone buildings with corrugated iron ones.

It being Sunday, families were returning from church, all dressed in crisp, starched clothing, the parents with their polished, gleaming shoes, the children minus them, following in a straight line, behind!

'*Karibuni, Karibuni,*' welcomed their host upon their arrival just on the outskirts of town. His family was a brood of considerable size as Mike, in tune with local custom, both erstwhile and modern, appeared to have acquired wives as readily as he had acquired businesses and wealth!

'Meet my family,' he smiled warmly as he introduced each of his three wives and the older children, the total count of offspring not being all present.

In a corner of the compound, under prior instructions, apparently, meat was being cooked on an open fire and the vegetarians were ushered quickly away to the veranda and patio to awaiting chairs.

After the eldest missus arranged soft drinks for the ladies, she brought a whole basket of fruit. 'I understand you are fasting; this produce is from our farm at Limuru in the highlands. Pears, plums, apples all grow there in abundance. When my husband acquired the place from a *mzungu* farmer, there was a running canning factory but the demand for fresh fruit is such, we closed the factory and it has proved even more profitable.'

Mike discussed figures over beer with the gents, sitting in the garden, a huge lawn area with flower borders. A few guests arrived; a European farmer from the adjoining *shamba*, an Indian professional who was clearly the family accountant.

Expounded the host, 'Sharma, here looks after all my accounts and also those of my wives who have a couple of small businesses of their own. He knows more about my money than I do,' he chuckled.

After a while, a couple of African dignitaries arrived, one of whom was clearly recognised as the Agricultural Minister. 'You're moving in high places,' whispered Uncle as he took Mike aside.

'Oh, I knew some of these guys before, but the ties have been strengthened since I made my grade in the business world, all thanks to you,' he responded, mock punching his one-time benefactor, now more of a friend, affectionately.

There was talk of a new era, with all races living in harmony.

Said the eminent guest, 'A number of foreigners, have left, but there is no reason for all races to follow suit. Despite the non-citizens awaiting departure, those taking up citizenship and the businessmen should do fine in a new and prosperous Kenya.'

By the time dinner and fruit salad dessert – prepared from their own fruit, of course – was over, it, was quite late in the evening, and the guests all said their good-byes. The ties of friendship with the Vakils remained for a long time to come and Mike was a frequent visitor to both the office as well as residence of the family.

Chapter 24

Week end at *Shamba Yetu* (Our Farm)
... digging graves past ...
playing Sherlock Holmes!

Shekhar's love of all things nature-related meant trips to the countryside and he endeavoured whenever possible, to get out of the capital and visit upcountry, as he did in the early years, in Mombasa, when with family or friends the north or south coast were the destinations for weekends. Now that the family had moved to the capital, included were such haunts as the hotel at Lake Naivasha, Mount Kenya and its Safari Club (courtesy of the Hollywood film star, William Holden) and safari lodges.

In addition, there were a couple of farmers known to his friend Dilip's maternal uncle who had their farms not too far out of town. One such was a Greek farmer who owned *Shamba Yetu* (Our Farm) near Ruiru, a small farming town, halfway between Nairobi and the town of Thika, which is approximately thirty miles north of the capital.

On weekend, after the short rains of October had subsided and the weather was warming up, *Mamaji* and co decided to accept the invitation from his friend Andrios Kariaku and make their way towards Ruiru. Their host had, since acquisition, developed his place and how! Coffee, fruit, poultry/eggs, limited livestock and vegetable produce abounded; a large portion was distributed for sale and some to Nairobi.

As they approached the farm, Shekhar asked, 'I suppose there aren't many of the original owners, the English settlers, left then?'

Mamaji who, as we know, was an expert on Kenyan
history replied, 'Well, as far as farm owners are concerned most have left, the farms having been sold or
surrendered under the government's Kenyanization
policy to the African and others, sold to the likes of our
Greek friend Andrios. Of course, those who were in
administrative work have nearly all departed, not
wanting to work under the natives. In the case of surrendered farms, apparently, the British government
compensated the departing farmers.

Dilip joined in, 'And as for the *wahindis or banyanis*
(Indians) they fall into various categories as well.'

'True,' said their elder. 'The ones who opted for British
citizenship will soon depart to the UK,* whereas citizens
like myself will remain as will professionals, like you
chaps.'

He reverted, 'As you probably know the white settlers
who had become masters, occupied and farmed the best
of the land, which was the highlands. Traditionally, the
Kikuyu tribes owned these and the struggle for independence and the *Mau Mau* rebellion was sparked off
simply by the desire to regain what was rightfully
theirs.

'Our Greek friend had purchased this farm from a
British colonial; however, the sale took place a few years
before independence as, apparently, the latter was getting on in his years.'

When the trio arrived on Saturday mid-day their host
was waiting and received them in the front garden of his
farm-house. The two friends had known each other for
years but not met for quite a while and their standard
greeting was: Ambros: *'habari za siku nyingi Banyani?*

---

* in what came to be known as the Asian exodus.

(the slang for Indian or Bania). *Mamaji*: 'sawasawa
Kariyuki' (it so happened that their host's surname
Kariaku resembled a common Kikuyu surname *Kariu-
ki!* And that's how his friend called him often). They
embraced.

The farmer was tall and sturdy, sporting a thick moustache. From his rigid features one could see he had
toiled hard at the land. He smiled warmly at the two
young men and after exchanging a few pleasantries,
they explored the farm and had tea on the veranda. The
guests had a good look at their lodgings, the house
boasting four large bedrooms. They reckoned the original owners had guests often, staying overnight, what
with their weekend carousing and parties. Wooden
floors considering the cooler weather in the highlands
and countryside. Although this particular area was not
so extreme, the evenings certainly got chilly, especially
during the colder season. There was a huge kitchen
with furnace, gigantic living room with a few animal
trophies from those pre-conservation days and the real
delight of course was the veranda, patio and the garden,
sunken beyond, a lawn area and flower beds teeming
with roses, jacarandas and other flora on the borders. A
stream flowed at the end of the garden after which some
more grassland and then the fence to signify boundary
and of course keep livestock or intruders at bay.

At dinner, Mrs Kariaku introduced them for the first
time to the delights of Greek cuisine, moussaka and
other dishes.

She spoke in her sweet-sounding continental accent,
starting off in Swahili, 'Karibuni, bwana' and then,
'Gentlemen, I hope you like Greek cooking, yes? And the
feesh was caught by Andrios in the nearby river.'

The guests smiled and *Mamaji* spoke on their behalf.
It was however their discussions at coffee by the roaring
log fire lit briefly that changed the outlook of their

otherwise simple weekend outing. After discussing tourism, agriculture and the farm with the host, *Mama-ji* suddenly asked, 'How come the previous owner who still lives in Kenya sold out, especially when the farm business was thriving?'

Andrios looked at his guests for a long while, took a sip from his coffee cup and said, 'It's not a very happy story but I'll give it to you all the same. The ex-owner Edwards had the farm pass down to him in legacy, worked hard at it and purchased new land as well. However, with affluence came the lavish life-style, lavish parties, which the Nairobi and upcountry jet-set revelled at. There were rumours of adultery between Edwards and a wealthy socialite. His young German wife threatened to leave. She had friends in the south. Tanzania or somewhere.' (After the war, some Germans occupying the then territory of Tanganyika, moved to Kenya.) Their host paused to extinguish the fire as it was getting warm in the room. The younger two guests were all ears for the rest of the tale.

'Anyway, one night she suddenly disappeared. The servants said there had been one of their by now frequent quarrels and come morning the mistress of the house was not to be seen. The second car had disappeared too. The inquiry lasted for over a year. Edwards was the obvious suspect, but as no clues were found, and the passport and most clothing were missing, the police files were ultimately closed. Edwards appeared heart-broken, repentant. Just before the sale of the farm I had met him at a farmers' gathering and he took some of us aside, confiding that he felt his wife had taken a lover to spite him and something had gone wrong between them. Soon after, just before independence he sold the farm and moved to a Nairobi suburb.' Andrios finished and waited for comments, if any, from his friends.

Finally, *Mamaji* said, 'It does look like there was foul

play, although the police probably did not investigate enough. But after all these years ...?'

'But then how do you explain the missing passport and clothing,' Dilip asked

'Well, the simple, explanation would be, it was confiscated by the murderer to throw the investigation off guard,' replied his elder.

Although it wasn't very late, everyone seemed tired and they retired to their rooms upstairs. These had been graciously prepared by their hostess and were tastefully decorated, agreed all three guests. Sleep could not come to Shekhar, however. The window was slightly open and the curtains swayed gently to the breeze. He lay on his bed for a while but then, becoming restless, got up, lit a cigarette, blowing smoke into the night via the window which he now pushed open fully, and looked out towards the farm with rested elbows. Nearly pitch dark, it was not altogether silent. Underneath a crescent moon, the farm-workers were still active in their *nyumbas* (small houses/huts), smoke drifted gently from which, the workers, had given their final 'rites' to the *ugali* (maize meal), *posho* (beans), with *viazi* (potato) and the optional luxury, *nyama* (meat). The farm beyond, however, with the orchards and small fields seemed totally silent, contrasting with the barely audible Kikuyu dialect going on in the nearer lodgings.

All of a sudden, a scream pierced the night air ... It sounded like a girl's. As Shekhar could not see clearly from his window, not waiting further, he stubbed the cigarette and rushed out of the room and down the stairs, taking two at a time. By the time he reached half-way he was semi-bathed in perspiration and despite other noises could hear his own violently beating heart. Except for the hostess, the rest had followed him out into the night.

A young girl, obviously the daughter of a farm-worker

was ranting and raving in Kikuyu dialect. The young guests could not understand this tribal language beyond the greetings stage, but the uncle with his long years all over the country spoke it quite fluently.

For a few seconds, Shekhar looked up to the sky and the crescent moon and then silently and fleetingly shared his thoughts with his friend, both thinking alike. One had heard of a full moon night causing havoc, but here it appeared to be a different story. Presently they returned to their lodgings, where their host, observing their perplexed expressions began to elucidate, referring mostly to the uncle, as the latter had spoken to the farm-workers in detail in their dialect.

Soon after Mrs Edwards had disappeared, the young girl who was a maidservant and close to the mistress of the house lost her speech. Every now and then she hallucinates, apparently in memory of her departed mistress. The workers have tried their own methods including witch doctors without success. Everyone was silent for a while. At length *Mamaji* said, 'About the inquiry, I mean, everyone suspected the husband and I gather from the farmhands albeit reluctantly, their frequent quarrels were known to all, including their social circle.'

Looking at the younger men he posed, 'If you were the murderer where would you dispose of the body?'

'Well, a lake or somewhere similar,' they answered. 'Yes, but there aren't any lakes around here. There are the falls at Thika – and the river Tana but that obviously would have been out of the question, because of the hotel at Thika and the Tana's open views. So, the obvious place would be a secluded ground spot. My bet is the no-man's land area behind the farm that's not been cultivated for years, as Andrios told me earlier,' he said, beating his fist into his palm.

'What about the second car that went missing?' someone asked.

Mamaji went pensive for a while and then said, 'I guess it was just a distraction, as the car was later found abandoned some distance from the farm. There was some torn clothing, suggesting some sort of attack by a human rather than animal as there aren't any wild animals in the area, being mostly cultivated land.'

The murderer had certainly tried to cover his tracks well in all ways possible and confuse the police and any investigators.

'Worth a try, that back area,' suggested Shekhar and Dilip, simultaneously turning to their host who was slowly and reluctantly being dragged into this Sherlock Holmes thriller-of-a-situation being developed before his very eyes!' But how could he refuse, and that too to his old friend of their bush days together.

Mamaji rounded off, slapping his thighs and concluded, 'Well, that's it then. *Kesho subui,* with the trusted farm foreman and your farm dogs. By the way, I also got the feeling that many of the older farmhands seem to know or suspect something which they did not wish to go into.' With these words, they retired for what was left of the night, but not before the curious friends asked *Mamaji* about his discussions with the farmhands.

The young men were impressed; 'You certainly are a bit of an all-rounder *Mamaji*, aren't you?' complimented Shekhar when he learnt that their elder spoke Kikuyu as well as Kikamba with fluency, and invited 'a bit of enlightenment would not go amiss.'

A bit of *atirere, okahaha* (Kikuyu greetings)

Mamaji relaxed on a settee and began: 'Well, the Kikuyu as you know are the prominent tribe here and despite many differences, some of their traits and characteristics are not unlike ours. For a start, they have a knack for trade and business, thus they are sometimes jokingly referred to as *banyani* Africans. They have the dowry system but in reverse; unlike our Patel *paithan* – he hinted at Dilip – it is the man who coughs up the payment to the girl's parents and along with cows and goats. Once again, like the Patel's original occupation they have been dabbling in farming and agriculture successfully. They have special marriage customs. A *kyuk* (lad) as they sometimes call themselves, has to prove his manhood rather like the Maasai by killing a lion. In what would surprise today's youngsters, they are rather modern in their approach even at rural level in selecting marriage partners as the sexes meet each other during group dancing and subsequently select suitable partners. Upon selection and elders' discussions and approval they have another curious ritual! The prospective bridegroom along with his friend kidnaps the bride and despite the pleas and screams of the girl no one, of course, intervenes.'

Shekhar chuckled: 'Rather like the Rajput trait of *haran* except that the kidnapping then was done single-handed!!*

Mamaji gave a big yawn, 'Well, I could go on and on but we need an early morning start so we'd better turn in.' So saying, he bid good night to the pals.

The 'investigation'

When they crossed over to the other side the next morning, there were only two possible sights requiring investigation, as the rest was unlikely, open grassland. An area between two trees and covered in turfed grass, with stones spread haphazardly over a large area was selected as the dogs rushed towards it straight away

---

* For full reference see chapter 26.

and began sniffing and would not move away, scratching the earth all around. Three farm hands assisted. Their introduction by the host brought a much-needed smile on the faces of the guests in an otherwise sombre situation that had developed so soon after their arrival. Peter, Johnny and Michael were nick-named respectively – Peeta *kifaru* (rhinoceros), so called by his colleagues due to his pointed nasal features, Johnny *twiga* (giraffe), his uniquely lanky 6'7" frame, and Myko *manchesta* due to his tendency to burst into ungrammatical English from time to time!

It was almost lunchtime and getting warm with the sun overhead, in contrast to the chill of the morning when they had started out, when, finally, after much digging amidst perspiring bodies and aching hands, something was hit. What everyone saw upon removal of a wrapped-in-plastic-and-clothing makeshift coffin caused a stunned silence with the exception of their own heavy breaths and the soft trickle of the stream flowing nearby. The dogs, continued with their sniffing and were moved away by the host and a quick examination revealed the skeletal body and clothing. However, on the finger bone, a gold wedding ring was still intact; the killer had either been unable or did not have any gruesome means by which to remove this apparent evidence. After some deliberation, the police were called in and they contacted the relevant branch in Nairobi. Everybody wondered what would happen next; obviously, the criminal file on the husband would have to be re-opened.

Late on Sunday evening they drove back to the capital, in silence, and agreed to continue that silence upon reaching their respective homes, but not before having a chuckle about how the womenfolk would react were they to be provided with the details of their little escapade.

Andrios was in touch with the police from time to time

and the seemingly never-ending suspense came to an end, when after several weeks the trial was finalised. Edwards, the husband had pleaded guilty when confronted with the evidence, the background and motivation having always been present in any case.

All's well that ends well

The following week, Andrios gave a surprise telephone call to his friend and asked the three of them to share some good news, but only in person, he would not say any more. Arriving at tea-time and planning to return by dusk, they were straight away guided in by their farmer friend after the preliminaries.

The hostess' drawing-room where they were led to, found the former grooming at the mirror and a young African girl maid assisting her. They both turned around simultaneously and greeted them *karibuni*. However, it was the maid that took them by complete surprise, even astonishment for it was none other than Jane, the girl they had witnessed earlier, beaming at them and saying *'jambo bwana'* with her shy mannerisms. All three were stunned to see this transformation in the girl, who had appeared on the threshold of lunacy when they last saw her.

Sipping tea on the veranda, Andrios finally smiled and clarified to his friends: 'Everyone at the farm, after you left, kept inquiring after they became aware of the re-opened police investigations. The final news came as no surprise and they all rejoiced at the news. Apparently, the previous mistress was well liked by all of the staff, just as the present one is, I may add,' he smiled at his missus. 'Jane, the transformed girl you saw today, remained indifferent for a while, but presently with the other womenfolk and my missus explaining the events, came round to normality. It was as if justice had been carried out at last and her "Madam beautiful" as she referred to her erstwhile mistress was at peace in heaven above.'

Andrios finished his little tale and looked exhausted with the additional burden of the previous few weeks' events. Dusk was approaching and the guests prepared to leave saying their *kwaheris*, but not before inviting their friends to Nairobi and a promise to return, but not soon, they assured, knowing all at *Shamba Yetu* would need a period of 'recovery.'

As the Peugeout saloon sped towards Nairobi they could not help but reflect upon their last return journey, full of sombreness and question marks. *Mamaji* seemed to read his nephews' thoughts and distracting them from the outside view, the coffee fields on either side of the highway, teased: 'So, my dear nephews, fancy any more ... murder mysteries, then?'

Shekhar, in the front passenger seat, was silent for a while and then raised his knees to the dashboard, placing his folded palms behind his reclined head and replied: 'What I really fancy, my dear *Mamaji,* is a nice little break at the coast, at my favourite, Bamburi Beach Hotel, which I haven't been to for some time. Enough of the highlands for me, for a while, thank you very much!'

Chapter 25

Meri pyari Bahenia ... (My darling sister ...)

After all the excitement of the previous few weeks, Shekhar took his much-needed break at the coast. The workload at the office had meant that long breaks were on hold and now with a gap in sight, a few days away would not be out of order.

Dilip and family still lived at Mombasa and the friends had some social catching up to do.

The two friends had known each other since primary school days and it was no surprise therefore, that both spent most of their time in each other's company. During their younger days, if Shekhar had gone missing without informing the family, the first place to check would be Dilip's and vice versa. Geeta, Shekhar's sibling would often be found with them, as she was the only cousin in the same age group, except for Nilesh but then he had his own friend circle.

By the time they were in their late teens, the inevitable had happened. Geeta and Dilip were not just friends or best friend's sister/brother but had gradually begun falling in love.

Thus on this particular break Shekhar brought up the subject of possible matrimony since they were now well into their twenties and he had clearly seen the transformation.

He hinted to his mate, 'Dilip Kumar (he always called his buddy after the iconic Indian film star) if you wish to become my *Banevi/Jeeja Ji* (brother-in-law, sister's husband), you had better start taking steps. Mummy and Daddy have already started considering suitors.'

In tune with the times, most Asian parents remained in the dark, concerning their offspring's feelings unless the party in question 'spoke up' and the way Indian girls were brought up, in many communities 'love marriages' were a rarity, although things were changing.

In the event, it was *Badey Bhaiya* (elder/big brother) who had to do the honours and Shekhar and Geeta's parents approached Dilip's, who along with the son still lived at the coast. There was one little hitch, though. Dilip belonged to the Patel community and 'mathematically' simplified this meant, Patel + wedding = Paithan (dowry)! although the practice is discontinued in all but the rarest/conservative cases now.

'But surely,' exclaimed Shekhar, 'neither Navin Uncle nor Mummy Aunty (that's how he affectionately referred to Dilip's Mum) would bother to go into this kind of social … folly?'

His mate smiled wryly, 'Shekhu, you've only seen Mum's nicer side. Daddy might let go but with money matters, Mum will extract her pound of flesh from whatever sources or situations available.'

On his return to Nairobi, Shekhar conveyed the 'heavy' tidings to his parents and the next time they met after the parents had had their discussions, to the detriment of the girl's family, Shekhar showed his displeasure by his minimal conversation so the mum tried to justify herself; '*Jo Beta, vevaar ma to pehlethi chokhvat kareli sari, pachhi pachhalthi* … (look son in social/financial matters it always pays to be clear from the onset, to avoid bad feelings later).

Mamaji to the rescue

It seemed the lady was 'not for turning,' and Shekhar's parents were thus on the verge of complying, when Dilip had a notion, more likely a brainwave. *Mamaji*!! the one who invariably saves the day in such matters. Then there were others, more Swahili inclined, referring to him as the *Msuluhishi* (the peacemaker) since he was well known for resolving social tiffs. Shekhar remembered how this family elder took care of things and pacified him when he had had his first heartbreak.

He was, however still sceptical, 'Do you think Mummy Auntie will listen. She is the eldest sister after all, and in any case *Mamaji* is somewhere in Kisumu on business.'

'You just leave it to me, I'll drag him to Mombasa if I have to,' assured Dilip.

He was pretty sure of the outcome since his uncle's demeanour was such that no one in the family could refuse him once he had taken a stance. Sure enough, *Kanumama* arrived within a few days. He had been aghast when Dilip gave him the details over the phone earlier.

'What's wrong with *Motiben* (elder sister)?' he exclaimed. 'These ideas are getting outdated, in fact downright medieval, and to think that she is applying the same ideas to the Vakil's, despite our relations going back ages!'

He continued, 'I know *Jeeja ji* (sister's husband) won't utter a word for either side as per nature, but really ... Well, I'm coming to the coast in a few days and we'll sort this out.'

Dilip was over the moon and informed his pal accordingly. The 'showdown' took place at the weekend after *Mamaji*'s arrival. The unsuspecting sister had prepared a sumptuous meal but what followed, first gently but then in a rising crescendo gave her no less than a jolt, to put it mildly. The man took both husband as well as the missus to task and did not allow his *Motiben* (as she was the only one defending) past the ... 'But ... but ... Kanu (younger brother, so first name) we should at least ... But ... But' ... stage!

Finally, victory was proclaimed as brother asked sister to invite the other party to provide 'revised terms'!!

The wedding: lots of joy and a hint of tears

Indian weddings have invariably been an affair laden with pomp, fanfare and some ... tears of sentimentality, amidst the laughter and smiles and this one was no exception. On the day of the wedding nearly anybody and everybody who mattered seemed to have been invited and turned up. The bride looked stunning, the ladies took their opportunity in adorning themselves to the maximum and the gents did not lag behind with their smart, lightweight suits.

Mamaji and Shekhar decided to add a dash of old fashioned chivalry by hiring a horse for the groom, who looked absolutely a *Var Raja* (Majestic Groom) what with his silky attire complete with *Phento* (wedding turban)!! Dilip and his pal did not want to let go without a touch of thanks to their dear elder so amidst the proceedings, at a previously decided time they lifted their hero on their shoulders and rendered an appropriate comical song number from an old Hindi film, which went something like this:

Mama, O Mama, O Mama Mama Mama

Gharwalen khaye chakkarrrr (!) Tum to na khana chakarrrr (!)

O hamare pyare mamaaaa ... pyare mema!! ... O MAMA!!

(O dear *Mamaaji*, the members of the household – meaning especially Dilip's Mum – may go down in a daze, but don't you go down likewise!)

All well-wishers and insiders had a hoot at the apt choice of the song and its wordings. An unlikely embarrassed *Mamaji* pleaded with his nephews: 'Hey guys, *I am not* the one getting married – put me down!'

Finally, it was time to say farewell to the bride, groom and his family and the *jaan* (guests from the grooms' side)

After the smiles, it was time for a few tears. The most significant ones of course being those shared between father and daughter (daughter being daddy's girl, just as it is son being mummy's boy), plus in this particular instance, brother and sister. Among their entire brood Shekhar and Geeta had shared not a few special times together.

Their dear girl would remain in touch – it was only a few hundred miles between coast and capital; still, things would of course, never be quite the same ...

Who's next?

Matchmaking and attending weddings has been one of the biggest social pastimes among Asian elders.

One evening the four elders were holding discussions on their favourite subject recent and forthcoming weddings in the community when *Kakiji* commented. 'Now that Geeta is gone to her new home and our Nilesh too has turned double we have to turn our attention to the remaining eligible members.' Nilesh the sober elder cousin had recently married a homely girl chosen by the Vakil elders without any qualms.

Prafulbhai (*kakaji*) seconded the 'motion'. 'Reshma and Radha (the twins) are still young but we have to think about our 'prince'. The uncle always referred to Shekhar thus often spoiling him with gifts and more when his parents weren't 'looking'.

'So what say you, *mara rajkunvar*' (my prince), *koi rajkumari joi rakhi chhe ke nahin?*' (have you seen/found a princess or not?)

'Not so far, *Kakaji* but I'm open to offers,' replied the nephew cheekily.

'Very clever,' chided his aunt. 'We've recently had a couple of offers we're considering so unless you have someone in mind ...'

The elders all knew that the young lawyer would not allow himself to be pushed into anything. Nevertheless Dineshchandra (Dad) who invariably spoke in business-like terms commented, 'Well, young man, get your binoculars out and see if you can find the princess of your dreams, as time is running out ...'

Chapter 26

Love at second sight ...

The wedding season was in full swing. Consequently, the *Sanji*s (wedding dances) were also to follow with equal enthusiasm. The ladies were dressed resplendently in their purples and golden yellows, reds and blues, heavy sarees and all. It was Dilip's paternal cousin Madhu, who was tying the knot, so of course Shekhar had to be there and involved in all the proceedings (now that they were brothers-in-law as well as friends!). It was the month of November following Diwali and the short rains were over, the weather was getting warmer and after the mild upcountry 'winter,' silks and voiles abounded.

Manharbhai, the bride's father was a successful businessman in Nairobi and the friends lodged at his palatial bungalow in the Parklands Asian suburb of the capital, with the customary five bedrooms, a massive driveway plus gardens as you entered, as well as at the rear.

On the second evening after their arrival, an informal get together had been arranged. After dinner, someone suggested, 'Let's play *Antakshri*,' the musical game.

It was boys vs girls and when Shekhar's turn came, not being a possessor of silky vocals, he just spoke the lyrics instead of singing them, and that too in his slightly gruff voice, which made the lyrics sound sort of humorous.

'Foul, you cannot get away by just *speaking* the song,'

cried the lady sitting opposite him, but not before bursting into peals of laughter, which was encored by others as well. The lady checking herself apologized, half embarrassed. Shekhar could not help but observe her ravishing smile and her overall vivaciously attractive persona. He hunched his shoulders, 'Sorry, but that's the best I can do.'

'We'll let you off this time,' said the girls, looking at the other more musical members, but the die had been cast and Shekhar could not stop himself from glancing in *that* direction several times that evening. By the time the game finished it was late. Only a select few remained and Dilip, when they had a moment alone, reading his bosom friend's mind said, 'By the way, that is Shila, a close friend of Madhu.'

'Who?' pretended the other.

'We both know who,' came the knowing reply but by then coffee had arrived.

Since the group was now small, there was opportunity for more shared conversation. They moved out onto the veranda, some relaxing on the sofa-swing popular among Asian families in the tropics. Initially there was small talk about the earlier evening proceedings and Shekhar managed to step on the opposite party's toes; placing them at cross-swords at every turn, it seemed.

'Rather spicy, those *Kachoris and Bhajias*,' said most of the men. 'And the *service* by the ladies could have been better,' quipped Shekhar as well as his pal, cheekily.

'Absolutely,' a couple of the others joined in.

Apparently Shila did not agree and responded immediately. 'Oh I think the items were all fine and so much effort ... what do you say, Geeta?' Then continuing, 'and the men could do some helping in the kitchen for a change,' she finished chiding with a smile, but making her point all the same.

'How feisty,' thought Shekhar, 'another plus point.'

There was more toe stepping when the pals made a comment on one of the guests, but then as the conversation changed and moved from one subject to another, Shekhar found to his amazement as well as delight that the lady in question shared his own passion for western Hollywood movies and the great outdoors of which there was no dearth in Kenya. He made his move. 'At last we find some common ground.'

'Well, you never know, there may be more,' she replied, but still matter of fact.

Finally, conversation centred round the game of cricket, and it was only Shila among the ladies who participated with equal enthusiasm as the men, and as the pals were aware, few ladies, unless they have lived on the sub-continent, seem to be infected with this mania.

'Shila used to be our netball captain during high school days and also excelled at athletics,' informed Madhu to the group. Turning to her friend she laughed, 'With all that energy you have built up over the years, you always look all set for the *saanji garba* which are due, tomorrow night.'

Not to be outdone, Dilip spoke on behalf of his mate, 'Shekhar may need coaching in singing, but he is a master of the drama and stage and was our star batsman for the school cricket team.'

Everyone was smiling, as, for a while it seemed there was some sort of match-making attempt going on and to break the embarrassed momentary silence, Shekhar cleverly intervened, 'What I really need coaching in at present, is the *Dandias* (stick dance). Any volunteers?'

'Oh, I'm sure there'll be many,' laughed Shila, not wanting to be pushed into anything.

It was quite late by the time everyone retired for the evening and Dilip was observing his pal as they flopped down on their beds after the day's hectic social proceedings. The tornado that was raging inside him was quite apparent to the other. Almost a decade after his high school heartbreak and for the first time since, something very unusual was stirring inside him ...

The morning sun pierced through the window curtains in the rear bed-room where they had boarded, casting shadows. The cockerel cried, sparrows chirped and Shekhar reminisced over the previous night's events, staring at his friend's still-snoring frame. He suddenly heard voices in the garden outside and peeping out of the window saw the ladies plucking flowers for the prayers. Showering quickly, he dressed in his smart casuals, wanting to look respectable and ventured out. The garden was large, by local standards, with roses and jasmines dominating the borders, which he began admiring.

'Join us for breakfast in a few minutes,' invited Madhu.

The thought of an Indian breakfast with *Masala* tea, spicy *Puris* (Indian fried bread) among other items made the young man hungry, but more enticing was the prospect of sharing a few words with the hostess' friend. Shila, unlike the previous evening's more sombre saree-attire, was dressed in a Punjabi dress, all white with subtle embroidery, adorning simple jewellery and perhaps befittingly her medium-long hair tied into a bun, tall and elegant, and looking even more attractive in her simplicity. She was about to pick a rose.

'Allow me,' Shekhar offered and then could not help himself, 'that's a "morning star" by the way.'

'Really?' she mocked, widening her eyes.

Undeterred he named a couple more, and waited for her reaction, tongue in cheek.

'Very impressive. I suppose this is one more of your "special" talents!'

'Well, actually, Dad's best friend is a flower connoisseur,' confessed Shekhar, referring to uncle K.K., 'and being an admirer of all things beautiful and natural, I pick up a few hints here and there,' he was being both candid as well as quaint.

The lady seemed impressed by the guilelessness, perhaps in contrast to some of the other young and quite pompous fellows doing their usual bit, showing off to the opposite sex in the middle of all the serious proceedings.

At tea, Dilip teased, in whispers of course, 'Who's really getting married then?' having realised his man had gradually fallen head over heels in love. 'I haven't seen you this way, since we left high school and certainly never during college. Mind you though, she's a tough one, that Shila, you'll need all the help that cupid might offer,' he chuckled.

'She appears to be *Punjabi*,' his friend commented. 'I noticed, among other things, a touch of what appears to be her own dialect, when she had invited her friend with the expression, *'Tamey badha avo chho naa?'*

He continued, 'It's nice to observe though, in Nairobi, just as in many other parts of the country most Punjabis and Gujaratis speak each other's dialects fairly fluently, right from school and after hours play contact, to housewives as well as the menfolk.'

By the time Shekhar drove them all to town later to make some final purchases for the wedding, the object of his affections had thawed considerably and they talked of nearly everything under the sun, including relationships and marriages!

During *Saanji* later that evening everyone danced long into the night, under illumination both natural as well as manmade, which gently brightened the rear compound, witnessing the dance frolics both the female *garba*, the male *garbi* and the *dandias,* Shekhar having received his 'coaching', simple though the manoeuvres are, from more than one seasoned player.

When they fell into the customary groups of four, Dilip

who was a consummate dancer dragged his chum along opposite Shila and Geeta, and the fervent pupil picked up fast, managing to impress the ladies.

A couple of unfamiliar faces appeared among the players. Madhu, playing nearby seemed slightly perturbed, 'I think there are some fellows from the neighbourhood. Although most are nice and civilised, there's always some rotten egg who spoils the party; I think this one always hangs around with some ruffians from outside the community.'

'Don't pay attention to them,' assured Shekhar, as usual calm and unruffled. His motto was never think about a situation, especially like this one, until actual occurrence.

They were presently joined by other dancers, who apparently fancied themselves as ladies' men. One of them approached the girl partners wanting to intervene. When Shila responded by ignoring them, they nevertheless persisted.

Shekhar intervened, 'Excuse me friend, but the ladies are our dancing partners, could you move?'

The reply was a sudden punch to Shekhar's face.

Totally unprepared, he nevertheless recovered quickly and raised his fists, never to back away from a fight, but then restrained himself, as he did not want to turn this into a brawl.

Wiping his mouth with the rear of his hand, he said, 'Look friend, if it's a fight you're after, step outside and we'll finish it there.'

However, several men folk from the hosts intervened, sent the outsiders away and stopped the situation from getting out of hand.

The ladies noticed simultaneously as Shila said, 'You've got blood on your lip.'

'Oh, it's nothing, thanks,' Shekhar said disarmingly, with a wave of his hand and a smile.

The object of his defence, however, without a moment's hesitation moved to her belongings which had been kept aside during the dance, and returned with a 'kerchief.

'Oh, don't bother ...' began Shekhar.

However, in full view of a young as well as elderly audience, the lady wiped the traces of blood from her chivalrous defender. They looked at each other for a few seconds, ignoring the knowing smiles all around them, their eyes doing the talking, and then finished the dance ...

The wedding itself was a lavish affair, full of pomp and show, as generally Indian weddings go, held at one of the capital's big venues with a guest list running into hundreds. Sending off the bride by late afternoon, tears and all, it was time for the guest entourage to say their goodbyes. They made their way to Parklands to collect their belongings. After their short but happy acquaintance everybody, at least in the bride's camp, was a bit emotional.

Dilip, however winked at Shekhar and then looking skywards began whistling Presley's *It's now or never*!

The prospective hero of the hour somehow fumbled. During college, he had known girls, sure, but after Rita, he had sworn never to get anything past the most casual, in a relationship or friendship.

'But here it is love, pure and simple; well perhaps not so simple,' he thought to himself.

He approached Shila and began, 'Well, looks like all good things have to have an ending, unfortunately. It's been ... um ... good ... By the way, thanks for the *dandia* lesson,' was about all he could muster.

'It's OK,' laughed Shila.

'Idiot!' whispered his pal from nearby. 'Is that all you can think of to say?'

The families were loading the gear. A minute or two and she'd be gone. 'Mm ... perhaps ... we could ... meet again?' he ventured at last.

She was straight-faced for a few seconds. 'Yes, she *is* a tough one alright,' he remembered what his buddy had said.

'Madhu has my number,' she said finally, with a smile that was subtle yet eloquent.

When the vehicles began to depart, Shekhar thirsted for just one more signal, wondering ... 'will she or won't she?' ... 'will she or won't she?' ... And then, just as the car turned at the junction, the lady threw a final glance backwards, and waved, yes, just a restrained wave, but one that confirmed his feelings. And in those few moments, Shekhar Vakil knew finally, his heart was lost for all time to come ...

The lady acknowledges ...

The next few weeks were hectic at the office. New clients had been signed and there was just no time for social activity, leave alone romantic liaisons! When things had cooled down a little, and Shekhar was going through his diary, one evening, there was a call from Dilip. After the usual pleasantries he said, 'Madhu is in Nairobi, I met her a few days ago.' If you have no other plans, we're going on an outing upcountry this Sunday, the newly-weds are here only for a few days. you can join us. And listen, you know who, will also be there.'

'Well that sure was a pleasant surprise, to say the least,' thought the other and accepted the invitation.

Sunday was bright and beautiful, perfect for a picnic. They had decided on 'Fourteen Falls' outside Thika, the small industrial town, a most popular site. Two vehicles were taken and Shila drove one of them with the girls and a couple of friends as passengers. They passed Ruiru, home of Tusker beer and Kiambu with the coffee farms and Kenya breweries respectively, finally arriving at Thika, home of the sisal farms and bag factory as well as the pineapple farms and canning factory.

'Let's have some pines,' someone suggested and they stopped by the roadside vendors, who sliced the fruit, often in chunks dripping with the juice. Shekhar obliged and passed the fruit round.'We'll spend a short time at Thika or Chania falls and have tea at the hotel,' the men suggested. The entourage of ten alighted at the site and Shekhar met Shila after what seemed to him, to have been an eternity. Dressed in levis and a short-sleeved top with sunglasses and earlier seeing her confident manoeuvres behind the wheel, he could well imagine her prowess on the sports field, a far cry from the traditional Indian restraint and the garb she had adorned at the wedding proceedings.

After the pleasantries, he said apologetically, 'I had meant to phone, but we were drowned in paperwork, how have you been?'

'Oh, I've been pretty busy too, what with the tourist season picking up,' Shila referred to her job as a travel company manager.

'Anyway, thanks to our friends we meet again,' he said without any pretence.

They talked about the area and country in general, 'We pass this sight quite often, I have relatives at the twin towns of Nyeri and Nanyuki,' she said.

They all made their way towards the falls, admiring and exhilarated by the cascade with its substantial drop. The younger members took the steps leading to the bottom to get a closer view, which forms River Thika/Chania.

Back at the hotel for tea, Dilip said, 'Great spot for a short visit outing and yet ...'

'And yet what?' asked Madhu. She looked relaxed and happy in the company of her new husband. Married life seemed to have started off well.

'Well, apparently, a prominent doctor's wife chose this spot for suicide.'

'You mean she drove all the way here and ...?'

'God Almighty!' exclaimed Nalini, another friend.

'Well that's the way the story goes, but let's think of happier things and make our way to the "Fourteen".'

It was still early afternoon when they arrived at their destination.

'What a breath-taking sight, I never tire of coming here, and can't think of a better place for an outing so near to Nairobi,' said Shekhar marvelling for the umpteenth time at the fourteen parallel cascades with their huge drop, creating pools at the bottom and then the river, part of the Athi flowing on.

On the banks at a distance, cars were parked as people unloaded their picnic hampers and crates of beer and cola which were shoved into little pools and nooks of cool water, further protected by the shades of huge trees with their extensive, drooping foliage. As the *Khichdi* and veg. or chicken *Masala,* the two most popular culinary items were cooked on open fires, depending on what took your fancy, the younger members ventured out, first having collected firewood and then to just look around, despite previous visits. All around, family members indulged in card games, siestas after meals, singing(!) and ball games following into late afternoon.

After lunch and a few rounds of rummy, Shekhar glanced towards Shila and offered, 'fancy a stroll?' The lady hesitated, but only for a second's glance towards the others and then beamed her assent.

'There's no wildlife around, obviously, but super bird life abounds on top of the scenic beauty. Did you know,' he continued with a grin, 'they did some Tarzan film shooting here? Although it was years ago, or perhaps, it could have been at the seven forks falls around the market town of Fort Hall, off the Nairobi-Nyeri road.'

'You love this country don't you, Shekhar?' she posed, looking at him not without admiration. Here was a guy, cool and collected, artistic and compassionate and yet could be tough when the situation called for it, like when he had defended her honour at the dance. Perhaps both were thinking the same thing. Just as he had not known a lady feminine yet feisty, with all-encompassing interests, she too had yet to come across a man like him. She had called him by name for the first time, and whatever little barriers there existed, were breaking down ...

'Absolutely, Shila, and I've gathered you do, too. The *maasis* and *kakas* (elders, uncles, aunts) have their own reasons, the lifestyle and business opportunities, so it's a bit disconcerting to hear about the impending Indian exodus to the U.K. Hope we do not have to follow some day, but who knows?'

They had ventured out quite a long way from their group, so Shila, with sudden realisation, teased, 'Come on Mr Tarzan, they'll be sending a search party out if we don't turn back now,' and with a mischievous smile she guffawed, 'wonder what you'd look like in a loin cloth, an Indian Tarzan?'

'Well, madam that actually would be Zimbo, the poor man's Indian version,' he informed.

Her sparkling eyes were too much to resist and of course he absolutely adored her special teasing, lively demeanour, so he just had to respond further, kneeling into the water flowing nearby and splashing her with, 'OK Jane, whatever you say, Tarzan obey.'

'Ouch, that's cold,' and she impishly splashed back and made a run with him in pursuit. When he caught up, she was laughing away, catching her breath, with care-free abandon, reminding him of their first encounter at the wedding. He did not stop until very close, looking deep into her eyes. There was a storm brewing in them that he had not seen before, never in fact in any girl. They were still not too far from the waterfalls and the odd droplets fell on her face, her hair slightly dishevelled and fluttering in the mild breeze.

For the first time, she could not meet his gaze, her face slightly reddened as she dropped her eyelids. Her utter femininity and transformation totally overwhelmed him. 'So this is what love is all about,' he mused to himself, 'and what women do, to bind their men to them, enslaving them by their very act of *apparent* surrender!'

They were quite alone now, with voices in the distance, and the sun going down, perhaps signalling him to take his little opportunity. He gently took her face, a rose in bloom, into his palms (... *Mere hathon men tera chehera tha, jaise koi Gulab hota hai ...**) covering its entirety with gentle kisses, taking her petal-like lips, then her mouth as she yielded them completely, tightening her palms around his wrists and then slowly her arms around his neck, as he took and held her in passionate embrace ...

Realising it was getting late they made their way back briskly, knowing eyes and grins, all awaiting them. 'What have you two been up to and when did all this start, asked the recent bride, slapping her friend on the wrist.'

'Ask your Shekhar *bhai,* he has been after me it seems, since we beat them at *Antakshri* the other day,' replied Shila, looking at her man with mischievous accusation.

'Well, we all agree you two do make a perfect couple,' approved her friend.

Dilip, however brought a touch of realism to the otherwise light-hearted discussion. 'Now it's only the final hurdle left. *Ashirwaad* (blessings) from the parents!'

Most in the group knew what that meant. Pleasing the

---

* I held thy face in my hands, as I would, a Rose.

conservative and unbending individuals among both the parents; in Shekhar's case it would four of them, with *Kakiji* the hardest nut to crack!

'Hold your horses everyone, he hasn't even proposed yet,' said Shila audaciously.

'Well I'm certainly not going to risk it here, and there's time enough later,' replied the opposition.

'You hope,' said the lady and amidst the ensuing laughter everyone made for the vehicles as it was twilight by now.

The proposal ... and the reaction!

For the next few months the two met as often as was possible, but somehow the man was in no hurry to pop the four-word question.

One Saturday afternoon as they relaxed at a country hotel, one of their favourite meeting haunts, just outside the capital, Shekhar seemed to be in a romantic mood. They were in the landscaped grounds, and he lay, with his head on her lap, her long, slender fingers running incessantly through his hair, doing what women in love apparently tend to do. He seemed to be on the verge of saying something and yet holding back.

'What?' she asked.

Even at such a time he could not help expressing himself in Swahili, his coastal roots coming to the fore every now and then. '*Mama, bona una onekana saafi sana leo?*' (Madam, how come you look so pretty today?)

'All this pure Swahili of yours, perplexes me at times, you'd better start giving me *private* lessons,' the lady responded naughtily.

He translated and at last gave words to his real thoughts: 'It's true what the poet said, and I regret it wasn't I who wrote it, for it is at times like these that I wish I had inherited my ancestral profession; certain things just cannot be said in everyday terms.'

'Have a go, nevertheless,' she said, 'I'm all ears.'

'Well, you can't expect an exact repetition, but I will do my best and in my own simple wording.' He cleared his throat. 'Having thou in my *arms*, has given me the realisation that the wealth and heavenly happiness of the entire world has landed at my *feet*' ... (*Tumhey meri banhon men paa kar, ye mehesoos hota hai mujhe, jaise ke saari duniya ki daulat aur jannatmai khushi mere kadmon mein aa giri hai ...)*

'So, you dabble into a bit of Urdu as well? ... Anyway, I'm most flattered, anything more?'

He hesitated for a while. 'Can't remember the rest, but there's something else I want to say, less poetic maybe, but much more original.' He looked at her seriously for a while and finally came out with, 'Shila, I want to spend the rest of my life with you, be my permanent friend and companion, the mother of my children, the grandmother of my ...'

The lady stopped him in his tracks. 'Hey Hey Hey, just ... one moment, Vakil Saab, if it's a proposal, which it sounds like, please do it properly; the kids and grand-children can come later ...'

And so it was, that under a fading African sun that evening, Shekhar Vakil got up, then went down on his knees and asked his lady love properly, whether she would become his 'lawful wedded wife.'

And with eyes almost brimming, she replied, 'Yes, of course I will, you idiot, I was afraid you'd never ask!'

The elders' approval and blessings were required and Shila's father and Shekhar's *Kakiji* were the biggest obstacles. Shila's father had his business partner's son in mind for his daughter and no little furore was caused at her home. 'Well, looks like I will have to perform your

Haran,' said Shekhar only half in jest.

'Please be serious, Shekhar, my dad will not relent.'

'I can now see where all that robustness comes from, daddy's girl, but I'll have to put on all my charm onto my Mum, Dad and the others and see if there's a social link somewhere to convince all round. And if not, I'm prepared to create hell and high water.'

When *Kakaji* and *Kaki* plus parents came to meet and see the prospective bride, a meeting was arranged at Manharbhai's, Madhu's father as he also had connections with Shila's family.

The idea was to convince the groom's parents which would leave only Shila's father as hurdle. On the chosen day Shila was dressed in her best traditional attire, looking all radiant and charming. Touching the feet of her elders and acting demurely for a change, gave her future husband a chance to create mild mischief.

Both the mums were easily won over and after a brief talk with the prospective bride, *Kakiji* too, her customary hard features relenting.

'*Arre*' Shekhar, how did a *booddhoo* (buffoon) like you manage to ensnare such a princess?'

Everyone laughed at Auntie's little quip. Although she showed it rarely, Shekhar did happen to be her favourite. Since the last bastion from his side of the family had broken down, the nephew saw no need for any formalities

'Don't go by her put-on conduct, *Kakiji,* it is she who chased me.'

Shila went red with embarrassment and began eyeing

---

* *Haran* – the noun simply means deer – the animal; Haran – the verb means something much more complicated. In the old days when a prince and princess from different states were in love and wished to unite in marriage against the wishes of the prospective bride's father/parents, the lady would write a love letter sent via a confidante (servant) and ask her lover to 'abduct' her at a pre-arranged time and place. Of course, when the 'enforced' father-in-law found out all hell would break loose resulting often in a battle.

her man as if to say, 'Just you wait and let me get you on your own!' She was just going to defend herself when he continued, 'Just look at my arms; she's a right bully, pinching me every now and then, when she can't get her way.' Everyone present burst into laughter.

'Mummy, *Kakiji*,' Shila, having won over her future in-laws, began her defence, '*Dekho na*' he has already started spoiling my reputation.'

Dad spoke on behalf of the elders, 'Well, we don't know who is bullying whom, but what we all agree on, is the choice of our fine, future *Bahu* (daughter-in-law).'

One matter still remained, and after much social politics and connections thereto, Manharbhai (cousin Madhu's father) managed to convince Sharmaji. Luckily, the mum and brother were already on Shila's side.

And so, exactly twelve months and seven days – as confirmed by Madhu, who was by now a seasoned wife – after her dear friend Shila and Shekhar had set their sights on one another at her wedding preparations, did they prepare to tie the knot ...

Wedding bells, settling down ...

The wedding turned out to be a grand affair as not only did the Vakils have a long list of invitees, the list from the 'opposite party' was equally long, if not more so.

Sharmaji had business connections as well as relations all over East Africa and he made sure, now that he had bowed down to his darling daughter's wishes, that not a single contact would be omitted.

The wedding reception was held at a very prominent and popular venue.

On the day, entourage for both parties arrived early as required.

The hall was almost overflowing with the invitees but

the groom's eyes were restless and it seemed he was on the lookout for someone.

Suddenly he rushed to the middle of the hall and shouted '*Mwalimu!*' Everyone's eyes moved towards the groom. The next second came the response in an equally loud, gruff tone '*Kumar!*' Yes it was his guru, Ali. They moved towards each other. Ali took his one-time protege in an affectionate bear hug almost lifting him from the ground. Shekhar's pals Dilip, Arif and a few others looked on with smiles and clapped; the rest of the crowd members looked on with perplexed expressions at this fifty-ish grey bearded, impressive looking African gentleman dressed in a smart suit.

'*Ame potea wapi?*' (where have you disappeared to) asked Sekhar slapping the arrival on his biceps.

'Ali explained he had been away and busy with his catering job. He then smiled and inquired, 'So you have found your princess at last!

'Yes,' replied the groom and asking Ali to wait he called his bride over and introduced her.

Shila smiled with a *Namaste* (Indian greeting), but Shekhar chided her gently and suggested touching the elder's feet, whereupon both of them did so as a mark of respect as per Hindu custom.

Ali was taken aback and became emotional too. Holding them both in his arms he kissed their temples saying '*toto yangu, vijana yangu*' (my children, my youngsters).

Presently the rest of the Vakil family came over and Shekhar insisted on Ali sharing their V.I.P. dinner table. There were of course surprised looks but Shila had been briefed by her man and she pacified her elders.

The other long-awaited guest was of course 'Dilip's *Kanumama*. He had come along with his other half (i.e. *mamiji*) and Shekhar after greeting them warmly took their elder aside along with Dilip and could not help asking mischievously '*Mamaji* is this *Mami* number one or *Mami* number two?!' (the youngsters always suspected – rightly or wrongly – that their elder had an African wife hidden away in some obscure rural town, as he had spent several years in the bush among the natives).

The wedding was a grand affair in all respects and everything was wrapped up by early evening as the groom and bride along with their entourage made for their new home together ...

The new Bahu was flavour of the month for all members of the family especially the twin siblings. Radha and Reshma simply adored their new *Bhabhi* and the newly weds had to exercise self control at times as the two 'hogged' their bedroom!

In time, the Vakils, as the new decade of the '70s approached, moved to a more affluent locality beyond the suburb of Westlands. Certain areas which were a colonial domain were now available to other races as the white population dwindled after Uhuru ...

Chapter 27

A new era

It was the decade of the 1970s. Subsequent to Uhuru, many of the British colonials, farmers as well as admin job holders and Asians, who had opted for British citizenship, had departed. Some straight after independence, others during the late '60s at the time of the Asian 'exodus' and yet others, who decided to shift away after what took place in neighbouring Uganda, courtesy Idi Amin.

Professionals, businessmen and Kenyan citizens stayed on. The Vakils were one of them and made the most of their life style in the new environment.

Exploring the natural beauty of Kenya

In Shila, Shekhar had found the perfect soul mate who shared his enthusiasm for the countryside, among other interests as well and one of the 'nature trail haunts' that they embarked upon regularly with friends was the Western/Rift Valley Province.

One fine, sunny Sunday morning on a long weekend, they drove off in two cars. Shekhar and missus were accompanied by regular and old pals Arif, Dilip and spouses as well as two more couples who had fairly recently arrived from the sub-continent. During the '70s many Asian men, single as well as married, had arrived on work permits to fill the void caused by the departed.

Shekhar drove one vehicle with the male entourage making 'male talk' easy and Shila with the ladies who would all have a field day of gossip minus their menfolk! A couple of toddlers were accompanying their mums.

Leaving Nairobi, they drove north west towards the escarpment, signs of 'beware of falling rocks' met them on the left at around 20 miles and the tarmac road, built by Italian prisoners of the Second World War, as was the Italian church at the base – built out of scrap metal. At last, as they looked to the left they saw the floor of the Rift Valley as the land fell away.

'Gentlemen,' declared Shekhar to his enthralled foreign guests who were visiting for the first time, 'behold one of the wonders of the world, the Great Rift as we call it here in Kenya.'

They stopped a few miles along as the road began to twine downwards and had their picnic lunch at a lay-by before continuing. At last they reached a vantage point and stopped once more. What confronted them visually took their breath away. The guests stood speechless and looked at their host waiting for more detailed commentary.

Shekhar obliged. 'The Rift Valley, this gigantic fault or displacement in the earth's crust ranges from Nyasaland (as it was then known), to the Nile at the mouth of the Red Sea.'

'I've seen nothing like this, what a convulsion, the subsidence, whenever it occurred, must have caused,' exclaimed Mahesh Kulkarni, an accountant and one of the recently arrived expatriates, 'probably shaking half the world's land mass. The division it has caused seems clear enough to let the sea in, dividing, from what Shekhar just informed us, nearly the entire continent.'

'In fact,' added Arif, 'the Rift must have been a gigantic inland sea at one time, from which the waters have receded after the upheaval, leaving a succession of lakes at various places.'

The ladies soon joined them. 'Look,' pointed Shila to a group of local African men and women, dressed in colourful *kitenges* and *sukas*. They were keenly selling their attractive merchandise comprising of weaved basket work and wooden carvings representing animal figures, to other visitors. The expatriate wives were impressed and bought some items as souvenirs; someday if and when they went back to the sub-continent as *'phoren returned'* they could show the items to family and friends!'

Earlier Shekhar had pointed out the tiny villages below. 'These small villages house what will be the likely world champion runners of tomorrow according to the sports pundits as they sprint miles at a time to school and back on a daily basis.'[1]

'Another way of enjoying the spectacular views of the Rift, and they vary from time to time, are obtained by rail which follows the eastern escarpment as opposed to this western car route which will take us to Kisumu ultimately.'

'It is amazing how the valley appears and impresses itself upon the mind at various times of the day. The best times are, of course, like most of Africa, sunrise and sunset, the sky above striking with rainbow colour. Then at high noon the sun appears in a blaze of radiance with ship-like clouds sailing all around. Finally, the Rift changes its mood at twilight hour; you see the storm clouds and the whole valley appears uncanny, almost supernatural! The items which fascinate most are Mount Longonout an extinct volcano, and a favourite climbers' haunt; its old crater covering 24 square miles and it is easy to approach, tracked off the main Rift Valley Road. The Masaai nomad people with their

---

[1] Sure enough in today's marathons the number one positions are invariably occupied by Kenyan runners from the region!)

cattle and the teeming wildlife with the possible exception of the elephant, giraffe, zebra, buffalo – at Longonout and rhino at Mount Suswa.'

They were driving faster as they wished to reach Lake Naivasha for lunch, which is approximately fifty miles from Nairobi. The hotel is by Lake Naivasha and the grounds contain beautiful trees, shrubs and flowers. The lake contains a huge variety of birds, however, many were on crescent island, a private property. The entourage parked the vehicles and after a brief and impressive stroll ordered lunch which, as at most country hotels, was quite sumptuous. Afterwards they booked a boat for hire. Countless varieties of birds came into view and the guests became busy with their binoculars and cameras. Everyone was noticing the other guest Rajesh, a zoologist/biologist on contract with the Kenya government, on the go with his movie camera. His colleague, Mahesh, an Accountant laughed and commented, 'It's thanks to Rajesh that my missus and I came along, otherwise most weekends are spent socialising locally.'

Rajesh knew most of the birds by sight to the surprise and delight of the rest of the party. At Lake Naivasha, the greater variety of birds – over a hundred plus, different species – are available for the enthusiast to admire at Crescent Island, a private property. Permission therefore had to be obtained and was luckily granted. Dilip chuckled, 'I wonder if we would have gained access in the old colonial days?!!'

The zoologist commented, 'just look at how nature has created these creatures. It is as if an artist has taken a paint brush and intricately applied the various shades and colours!!'

They saw the utterly amazing, colourful saddle billed stork. The male has its large bill starting off red for a few inches, then changes black, then red plus yellow, neck is black, body wings top and bottom white feathered and in between green feathered and finally tinged pink in some part and the legs black-red!

The sacred ibis, coloured large black bill, neck and tail, in between body feathered white with tinges of yellow below the glossy ibis deep brown overall, including large bill with green feathers and wings, white tinge on head.

Shekhar, missus and the rest were most impressed with the scientist as any and every kind of artistry was always admired by them.

Shekhar was absolutely delighted and with his arm around his woman, complimented, *'yaar tum to bilkul apni type ke aadmi ho'*! (buddy, you are a man after my/our own heart!)

The night halt was to be Nakuru, the agricultural capital, and the fourth largest town of Kenya. During colonial times and to some extent later too the centre of the 'white highlands' as they were termed in the old days. Of course, there was also the Asian business population. 'It means dusty place according to the Maasai,' advised Dilip to their guests.

They reached just the outskirts of town, where Shekhar's *Masa* (maternal uncle) resided and where they were to put up for the night. Once again, the warm hospitality of the 'East African Asian' was evident in abundance.

It was dark but the family had waited. 'Welcome, welcome. We were about to have dinner and switch off the lights,' joked Masa.

Masi who had prepared a super, albeit simple Gujarati dinner smiled; 'nice to see you after such a long time, I hope your friends like Gujarati cuisine.'

Shekhar laughed 'Well, *Masi*, they don't have much of a choice, do they?'

The guests were from a different community and had come along and accepted solely due to Shekhar and Shila's insistence and responded to the hostess with a sub-continental touch, *'Masi amne gujarati bhojan ba-hooj pasand chhe'* (Aunty, we love Gujarati cuisine immensely).

After dinner, chewing Pan (betel nut leaves) and other mouth refreshments, the customary conversation went on far into the late hours, on the rear veranda, on the *hinchka* (couch-swing) under the moon and the stars.

As they prepared to bed down for the night, Shekhar took a final stroll into the medium-sized garden intermittently looking at the sky above and guest Mahesh joined him presently.

'Not ready for sleep yet Shekharbhai?' the latter asked.

Shekhar did not answer for a while, then said looking instead at his bosom buddy cum brother-in-law, 'Look above, Dilip Kumar (as he always called his chum) remember those light house days. Nearly two decades have passed since we used to play *thappo* and other adolescent pursuits in our half-pants underneath those stars. Nothing's changed *there*, but down here ... he circulated with his fingers ... a lot has changed. Uhuru, the exodus, Idi Amin ...' And then he pointed to the landscape beyond. 'That hasn't changed much either. But this ... and he pointed to the snoozing toddlers in their mothers' laps ... this is a big change for us.'

'You're talking in riddles and sound philosophical tonight, Shekhu,' said Arif who had surreptitiously joined them.

The reply was, 'All I'm saying is, I wonder if it's time for us to go as well. The East African dream as some have called it ... is it over for us?'

Maheshbhai immediately intervened, *'Arrey* Vakil Saab, don't say such things. If you talk of leaving, *hamara kya hoga?* (what will happen to the likes of us?)

Their conversation came to a sudden end as the hosts called them to retire for the night. Once again, the large hearted, warm hospitality came to the fore as the hosts offered to sleep on makeshift floor bedding, putting up the guests in the bedrooms, but ultimately the chivalrous menfolk slept rough and sent the family upstairs.

Shekhar reverting to his old charming self, teased, 'Our Shila ji is used to special comforts please ensure she gets the softest bedding.' The ladies burst into laughter awaiting a sharp response from the missus, but she was too busy with her offspring and merely eyed her man ...

Seeing the sights ... the Nakuru racing track

The following day the menfolk visited the famous motor car racing trek of Nakuru. Masa and his son (being Shekhar's cousin) gave a brief introduction, 'It is located at the lake view estate and the first races took place as early as in 1956. It is very popular and Kenya is known for its craze for motor sports, top of the list being of course the Kenya rally.'

The ladies went into town and did a bit of shopping. Upon return they packed a picnic lunch and visited the Lake Nakuru National Park.

The ninth wonder of the world?!

The cousin and guest Rajesh, the zoologist got along famously, discussing and explaining the inhabitants of the lake to the rest of the party. The guests were amazed to see the countless 'lesser' flamingos. Rajesh explained in scientific terms, 'during the rainy season apparently the water gathers in the low lying areas of the Rift Valley, forming seasonal lakes and minerals from volcanic rocks due to non-drainage passing onto Lake Nakuru and Lake Bagoria about 50km from here.

The hot water springs with the salty (sodium) water which are created from volcanic rocks contain bacteria which are food for these flamingos.

The ladies asked, 'but the water, it appears steaming hot! how do the birds ...?'

The scientists explained, 'It would appear nature has given a unique metabolism to the flamingos as their legs are able to withstand as much as 70 degree hot spring water and this has been going on since the creation of the Rift 30 million years ago! There are as many as a million, sometimes double that figure, birds gathered at this lake on some occasions. Like some humans, they are also "nomads" moving from lake to lake for feeding on the bacteria.'

Shila observed, 'they are so lovely and unique in appearance, pink feathered along with splashes of red, red legged and with black beaks.'

The cousin pointed out, 'look at their movements. This is the courtship dance; they go back and forth in lock-step movement along with their heads from left to right and back!'

The guests all seemed to agree it was certainly one of the most amazing natural sights they had ever seen ...

The scientist continued, 'perhaps an even bigger wonder is the gathering of the greater flamingos at Lake Elmenteita, these birds being taller and bigger than the other, smaller variety. Other fauna include thousands of white pelicans. You can see with their white feathers and (mainly) large yellow bills made this home from 1960 onwards. When their diet, a special type of fish was introduced at this lake. Also fresh water from river estuaries means they keep away from the hot water geysers which only the flamingos can withstand.

The national park is also home to both the black as well as the white rhino, buffalo and zebra.'

The group had their picnic and stayed until late afternoon. One of the wives of the guests was suitably impressed and pleased, concluding before departure, 'I wouldn't argue if this heavenly abode was given the title of the eighth or ninth wonder …'

By dusk it was time for the guests to make return tracks to Nairobi. Their hosts however, would not allow them to leave without supper which they had and said their goodbyes.

No *Kwaheri* yet …

A couple of weeks after their trip, the friends met for drinks at one of their common haunts in Nairobi, the Hotel Panafric. Towards the end of their meeting, Mahesh the accountant suddenly remembered *'Arrey, shekhar bhai hamari us din wali baat to adhoori rehe gai!'* (our talk of the other day remained unfinished).

Shekhar took a sip from his beer glass and looked perplexed, *'Kaunsi baat, dost?'* (what talk, friend?)

Mahesh reminded, 'Correct me if I'm wrong, but you gave the impression of making plans to leave us.'

Shekhar and Arif looked at each other and burst into laughter. Arif, the life-long friend knew his buddy's occasional whims and put an affectionate hand on the expat's shoulder. 'Maheshbhai, I wouldn't lose sleep over our dear friend's remarks. He does have a habit of coming out with such bombshells from time to time.'

Shekhar took his final sip from his Tusker (Kenya beer) and got up to move towards the parking lot, 'Anyway *mere dost* (my friend), if at all I do decide to leave this paradise which has been my home for over three decades I will make sure I give you no little notice. He paused and upon reaching the parked cars with a grin continued, 'Would a notice of, say, 24 months be enough?'

Books and sources referred to

1. *The Lion and the Lily – A Guide to Kenya* by Kenneth Bolton (1962)
2. *On the Threshhold of East Africa* by Lenore Reynell (1994) translated into English from the original Gujarati by Bhanuben Kotecha
3. *The Illustrated Encyclopaedia of Birds of Britain, Europe and Africa* by David Alderton (2004)
4. Internet Wikipedia (on Wildlife)

www.ingramcontent.com/pod-product-compliance
Lightning Source LLC
Chambersburg PA
CBHW050401030726
47503CB00006B/1957